Protectors of the Pure and Avengers to the Wicked

BARRY MYNES, JR.

LUCIDBOOKS

The Unlikely Conquerors: Protectors of the Pure and Avengers to the Wicked

Published by Lucid Books in Houston, TX
www.LucidBooks.com

eISBN: 978-1-63296-973-6
ISBN: 978-1-63296-972-9

Special Sales: Most Lucid Books titles are available in special quantity discounts. Custom imprinting or excerpting can also be done to fit special needs. Contact Lucid Books at Info@LucidBooks.com

May this tale become an eternal testament to
my precious family—etched in stone,
dedicated forever to my sweet, loving wife
and four precious little girls.

Contents

Foreword

I think it is amazing and exciting to know that my dad wrote a book about our family. The story can help me to be brave and strong in a scary time. I enjoy my dad's writing because of its adventures and the characters, especially Ybbub. I am proud of how hard my dad has worked on this book and for all of his dedication.

—Sophia Mynes
Oldest daughter, ten years old

Chapter One

Unwanted Company

Cruelly the thick winter blizzard had begun to blow. The sharp cut of the howling wind snuck through the small cracks of the tiny cottage walls. Pitched-together logs from the nearby forest with hay-filled mud 'twas the best Father could do for his family of six. Not in three decades had the heavens opened and graced this land with such heavy snow. Nonetheless, the sweet angels lay deeply asleep in their cozy beds, tucked in with warm, thick quilts stitched together from their father's old worn tunics and cloaks. No other use had they as each were filled with holes achieved throughout many of his mysterious adventures—most of which they knew little if anything about.

Their father marveled at each of them while standing by the door of their crowded room holding his half-melted candle. Fast asleep in one bed was Sophia, the eldest of the four, arms drooping off the bed, her knuckles close to dragging on the cold, dirty floor. As a barn cat rests asleep along the high wooden beams, this too was how she slept. In this case it was her long legs swaying back and forth and not a bushy tail waving uncontrollably. Dangerously flirting with falling off the beam and down onto the icy, dusty floor, it would indeed take a raging storm of a thousand hurricanes to awaken this young lady.

Straight across her lay what some would contemplate an angel, gracefully catching a night's slumber within those stitched quilts as a heavenly being on a puff of cloud. Her skin was smooth and as radiant as the spring sun, with freshly brushed hair draped along her pillow. In another tale her name would be Beauty, but it was chosen fifteen years ago to be Savannah. Due to her kindness and porcelain complexion, she was often referred to as baby Gene. While this sleeping angel was away, deeply lost in slumber, her father looked around to the other side of the room at the most coveted bed by the window. This young lady was rewarded with the most sought-after bed of the four, not due to their agreement on the matter but simply because no one would dare refuse her of it. It's been said that when anger emerges within her, the round, pretty face turns as red as a scarlet rose. A yell will then erupt like that of a molten volcano that some say can be heard clear to the next village such that of a bell ringing from a tower to warn of danger and harm to come. In that coveted bed by the window lay Scarlett Bell.

Four beds stuffed with wool from their sheep crowded this tiny, frigid, candlelit room—all occupied except for one.

He thought for sure that all was accounted for and tucked in safely asleep. But one remained amiss. She was regarded as the sweetest of all, some might say—Sarah Honey. Quietly he shut the door and tiptoed toward the staircase as each step exhibited the sound of squeaking boards and wood bending beneath his frozen feet. Twelve steps to the bottom of the staircase he cautiously went down to search for Honey. He observed a silhouette of Noel, his wife and mother of the four darlings, near the fireplace. Noel sat there with a warm glass of milk in hand and the other embracing that sweet child Sarah Honey.

"Now one last drink and it's off to bed you go," Mother whispered quietly. Her breath could be seen clear across the living quarters due to the snowy storm that blew just outside their cottage.

The fire had been much larger but unfortunately began to dwindle. "Yes, off to bed with you, my little, sweet angel!" he shouted while picking her up and then hoisting her high above his head, buzzing as if she were a bee.

Noel then shooshed him and said, "Be quiet. Weve already conquered the unimaginable. Do not wake the other girls."

He held Sarah by the hand, and they began to make the journey up the staircase with the glooming light of her little candle to see. As they quietly walked up the stairs, her father's scar on his left arm caught her attention. The scar was a mystery to her and the other sisters. Sarah debated with each step the decision to finally inquire how he had received it. She finally uttered, "How did you get that scar, Father?"

He froze atop step number eleven, almost making it to the top. Sarah looked up at her father as he gazed toward their bedroom door for what seemed eternity. As the candlelight flicked, flashes showed the most unsettling expression on his unshaven face. He then took a deep breath and sighed. "It's very late, my sweet angel. Off to bed you go." Kissing her on the forehead, he tucked her snugly into the cozy bed. "Now say your prayers and go to sleep."

As he began to walk out of the room, suddenly Scarlett rose straight up and mumbled, "Oh yes, please, I'll have another slice of cake." Then without hesitation, she fell back into her bed and began snoring. Sarah and Father looked at each other and giggled, both trying their best to remain quiet like a mouse. As he shut the door and gave a wink, he whispered, "Good night."

While holding the depleted melting candle, he looked down and observed the very scar Sarah Honey had inquired about. The flame cast such a glow that the wound appeared as if it had just happened. Staring down at it, his senses were lost deep within the unfortunate unpleasant memory of the day he had been cursed with it. The truth that lay within the scar was only known among his dear wife and a few more brave souls. Noel was not exactly given the entirety of the tale regarding the pain and unbearable suffering that was gifted on that day. He felt that her mind was too pure to entertain such corrupt, cursed thoughts.

Rubbing his eyes, he carefully walked back down the stairs, realizing he had completed the most difficult task of the day—getting the girls to sleep. Mother had now gone off to bed herself, hypnotized by the flickering of the lone flame atop the charred log in the fireplace. For her it was now an opportunity to catch what little rest she could get. It had been a day full of sewing, cleaning, sweeping, washing, cooking, and, most importantly, teaching the girls how to read and write. Father took it upon himself to pass down what he felt was most beneficial to the little ladies—how to spit, belch, climb trees, tie knots, recite silly poems, and throw a strong, right hook with their fists.

Two wooden chairs, chipped and worn down smoothly, now sat unoccupied near the stone fireplace. He crouched down and began to place several logs in the dwindling fire. No heat through the night on a winter storm of this magnitude would be costly, he thought. As one log slipped from his clutch and crashed brutally on top of the smoldering logs, sparks flew out and danced upon his left forearm, searing his skin. He swatted and raked off the coals from his now-cindered arm. A flicker of light then flashed above his head. He quickly looked up and realized it was the glow of the fire reflecting from the large blade that hung above the mantel. As the master of this blade, he had skillfully used it on many occasions to protect the pure and send vengeance to the wicked.

He carefully removed the sword from its place of rest. Staring into the sword, he instantly became lost within its blade. Each dent, scratch, and dark stain reflected an absolute truth—a truth that without each mark he would not have been alive to tuck his little angels into their beds. "It had to be done. There was no choice." Those words proceeded to echo in his mind as he held the great weapon of warfare.

The hilt was finely crafted from the purest of gold from the Kingdom of Golgrathia and complemented with a red jewel that was set at the bottom slightly below the wielding hand. The blade held many dents and scrapes, but the most noticeable feature was the point, chipped and blunt now after a horrific conflict many years ago. Just like the sword to him now, there was no point. Although incomplete, the scabbard had been lost many years ago while he was engaged in warfare—misplaced during battle that saw a few brave knights collide with the overflowing and rapid growing of evil.

Where could it be now? he thought to himself. Any knight would choose to have in his possession his sword instead of the scabbard, rather than the scabbard and not the sword. But what use would a farmer have with a sword now? "A mere relic of the past," he whispered to himself. But any knight would know that a sword is of no effect without the sharpness and readiness of the forged blade. Throughout all this time, he still had managed to keep it clean and ready. "Ready for what?" some may ask. Ready for the unknown secret that only he knew and desired to keep. Such things should be kept secret, hidden, and banished.

It was an evil so smothering that fright would linger within one's very soul just to hear the tale of it. It was one that still haunted and frightened even this once-brave, honorable knight. He then carefully lifted the sword from atop the mantel and held it in his rough, calloused hands. Feeling the edge of the blade, a sudden sting like that of a bee struck his thumb.

He looked down and saw a trickle of blood appear and mumbled, "Still sharp!" Amazed in unbelief, he thought begrudgingly, *Have I become too old to wield such a weapon?* Fear then began to overcome him. "Even as the sword keeps its reliability and sharpness, do those attributes remain for the one who has wielded it for so long?' Realizing it was far too late for such conclusions, the thought of his warm bed appeared to be more comforting. He then placed that symbol of strength and honor in its rightful place back above the fireplace.

After a quick scratch of the beard and a most overdue yawn, he began to walk past the front door. As he shuffled by, a thunderous knock boomed at the thick wooden door. His heart sank as he stood motionless as a statue. Standing quietly, he wondered who it could possibly be at this hour of the night. Their cottage was several miles from the nearest village. After all, that's how he liked it—peaceful and alone with his happy family. They kept to themselves, always busy with the horses, sheep, cows, and those menacing chickens—especially the roosters.

Cautiously he crept to the window where the only view was the thick blanket of snow flowing through the illuminated moonlight. It was too thick to catch a glimpse at who or what stood on the other side of the door. Knock! Knock! Knock! This time the banging included a clawing at the door and a chilling rattle of chains. Now there was no choice. The unknown trespasser was adamant, refusing to accept that no one was at home. The now farmer accepted the fact that it must be revealed who was at the door, even though he'd prefer not to know at all.

The dragging of chains across the rough, lumbered porch sent chills down his already cold spine. A heavy knock then followed, causing his heart to thump faster. Then there was a jolt at the door like that of someone ramming the gate of a castle. He then ran back toward the fireplace to retrieve his old tool of trade, firmly placing it in his nervous hands. No time to practice. No time to sharpen. Simply no time at all to debate within himself if he could still wield it.

The large, smoldering fire he had built blew out instantly as he ran to the door. "Who's there?" he shouted trying to overcome the choke of fear within his voice. A large force then budged the door open like a mighty rushing wind. As the snow blew inside and into his face, he shielded his eyes to try to get a glimpse at who wished to visit him on such a night and in such a manner.

The sword then left his clutch as it fell straight to the floor. The nightmare he carried as a curse that resided in his very soul was now staring him in the face. Gazing upon its dreadful horror, he uttered, "No! It cannot be!" A loud screech echoed into the cold, frigid house. With the door wide open and the nasty blizzard blowing inside, Father was there no more to block the evil that dwelled on the outside as any loving father would desire to do. The door was now wide open.

Noel, awakened by the loud commotion, ran to see what had happened. Scanning the area for but a moment, she whispered, "Daniel! Daniel!" Another loud shriek, and then Mother stood inside the house no more. In an instant, just as the burning flame of a candle vanishes, both Mother and Father disappeared into the blackness of the night.

Chapter Two

Hide and Seek

The eldest of the four girls felt the undesired kiss of winter on her cheek. Sophia woke up and realized that their tiny room now felt as if it were a block of ice. She began to wonder why it had gotten so much colder. *Father always keeps the fire going through the night. He never lets it just burn out*, she thought. Ever since she could walk, Sophia had often assisted her father in gathering firewood. She carried piles that were much larger than she was at the time and then worked her way up to even chopping the wood to bless her father with a well-deserved break.

Finally able to overcome the dread of unwrapping herself from the firmly tucked quilts, she placed her dainty toes down on the undesired frozen floor. "Savannah." No response. "Savannah. Savannah. Savannah Gene!" she yelled, followed by a throw of her pillow. The little angel then gracefully sat up, rubbed her eyes, and mumbled, "Is it time to wake up?"

Sophia responded with a most unpleasant "No! But wake up!" Savannah lifted her arms up and stretched with a yawn, causing her breath to be seen clear across the room. "Why is it so cold in here?" she asked.

"That's why I woke you up. Father must have let the fire die out." The two then got out of bed, draping their quilts over themselves to endure the frigid journey downstairs. "Go!" Sophia whispered quietly, not wanting to wake up the monster that was snoring across the room. "Hurry up!" Sophia ordered again.

Savannah turned around with the etiquette of a queen among her visiting nobles. She softly responded, "I am, Sophia. Please do not rush me."

As they crept down the stairs, the quilts felt as if they had lost their effect with each step they took. "Look!" Savannah said as she pointed toward the front door. "Why is the door open?"

The thick, heavy snow continued to blow forcefully inside. The fireplace and planked floor were now drenched with the cold, wet snow. The two empty chairs sat blanketed as if they had been freshly painted as white as the very wool inside their sewn mattresses. Both sisters, now confused about what had possibly caused the door to open, walked toward the entrance.

"Ouch!" shouted Sophia as she lifted her foot from the ground, jumping up and down on one leg. Savannah, seeing her in pain, rushed over to try to help her keep her balance. "What's wrong?" Savannah asked.

Sophia looked down and saw a long object coated with snow at her feet. She dusted it off with her foot and then noticed it was her father's sword. The sword lay there with an appearance of abandonment, lost from its purpose. "Father's sword," Sophia whispered. Both girls stood over the blade, staring while it lay on the floor. Curiosity and confusion overwhelmed them.

"Why is it off the mantel and on the floor?" asked Savannah.

The wind howled outside the door as they both gazed into the frightful moonlit storm. Nothing but the white of snow and blackness of the night filled their eyes as they stood there. A chill sent a shiver down Savannah's back. "Hey! What are you guys doing up?" Savannah and Sophia both screamed, startled by Scarlett looking down at them from the top of the staircase.

"Why is the door open, and why is Father's sword on the floor?" asked Scarlett. Sophia and Savannah looked confused and appeared unaware that they were still standing by the front door as the blizzard continued to funnel inside.

Then a soft, squeaky voice said, "Shut the door!" It was Sarah Honey, the last to wake up and attempt to investigate the mystery. "Mother is going to get very mad at you all for opening the door and letting all that snow in."

Sophia quickly looked at Savannah as if she had a great idea. "Yeah! Go get Mother and see if Father is in there asleep as well."

Trying to keep herself wrapped inside her quilt, Savannah

quickly ran to their mother and father's room. She opened the door and rushed to the side of their bed—a warm, cozy bed filled with pillows, blankets, and quilts, but that was all. The bed was unoccupied. Mother's slippers were still neatly placed at the edge of her side of the bed.

"They're not here! Mother or Father! Neither one of them!" Savannah yelled while standing bewildered at the foot of the bed. Then she heard heavy thumps of footsteps like a cow trotting through the house and up the stairs.

"Quit lying, Savannah! I know Mother's there. Stop playing your silly games!" As Scarlett and Sarah Honey urgently entered the room, they too saw the empty bed and puzzled look about Savannah's face. While standing in the bedroom doorway, they turned around and looked back at Sophia. "She's tellin' the truth. They're not here!" Scarlett replied.

The three girls then shuffled back to where Sophia was. Appearing as if she were frozen, Sophia's face showed no expression or hint of her thoughts. It was not that she was frozen due to the winter storm that covered her while standing near the door, but frozen because never had this occurred. Both Mother and Father were gone in the darkness of night.

"Sophia!" shouted Scarlett. All that Sophia could do was look down at the floor as the snow continued to drop on top of the sword, flake by flake. While each of the snowflakes fell, inside Sophia felt fear and uncertainty begin to pile up as well.

"Where's Mother and Father?" asked Sarah Honey while her lip began to quiver and tears flooded her beautiful blue eyes.

As her three sisters stood there waiting for an explanation or a reason, or somehow to justify why Mother and Father had disappeared, Sophia finally come back to her senses. "What? What is it, Sarah?" Sophia replied, looking at all three standing side by side.

"Where is Mother and Father? Where did they go?" Sarah repeated once again.

Sophia looked around the cottage, at the sword down on the ground, and back at her sisters. She said, "I don't know, Sarah Honey. I . . . I don't know."

Chapter Three

Alone All Together

Never had such confusion inhabited this small home deep within the forest. The cottage was on the outer lands of the Righteous Kingdom, defended by the glorious and brave soldiers of the Royal Golden Eagle Army, protectors of the pure and avengers to the wicked. All had heard Father quote that poetic saying all their lives but had no idea of the exact deep meaning it held.

Standing there, the three girls knew that Sophia was always with Father. All could agree that she knew him like the back of her hand. Chopping wood, shoeing the horses, or the rare occasion of going to the Kingdom's marketplace, Sophia was right by his side. If Father was needed for something around the cottage, Sophia would simply say, "What do you need, and I'll do it." If Father could do it, then so could she, all the while wearing her torn, raggedy dress stitched and sewn by her mother, Noel. While her resemblance to her father was obvious upon her reflection, that was not all she had inherited from him. Never did she back down from standing up for what was right.

Standing over the top of the sword, Sophia bent down to pick it up. As she placed her hand on the cold, frozen hilt, Scarlett let out a loud "No! That's Father's sword, and you know you're not supposed to touch it! I'm telling Father!"

Sophia then gazed outside the front entrance, seeing nothing but the snow and deep, dark blackness of the woods. Turning back to Scarlett, she said, "Hush, Scarlett! Don't you realize it? Mother and Father aren't here! We are alone! It's just us!" The room was silent. Nothing was heard but the violent howling of the wind whistling and brushing against the small glass window near the fireplace. Sophia dusted off the sword and picked it up from the floor. Holding it, she then stared at the blade while noticing her reflection as if it were a mirror.

Each dent, scratch, and stain caught her young eyes along both sides of the edges. The pummel was filled with notches of different sizes and shapes. The tip was unusual in that she never had noticed the chip at the very end of the sword. It was sharp on the sides but blunt at the end of the long blade. The hilt felt as if she were holding a frozen icicle due to the melting snow beneath her hand. It took all her strength to simply hold her father's sword. *What power and skill one must possess to be capable of wielding such a magnificent tool,* she thought.

While lost in its marvelous appearance but now desolate purpose, Sophia then heard a whisper like that of her father's voice in her ear. "Help! Olcnom. Oooolcnom!" The hair on her neck stood straight up as she looked around with eyes wide open. "Who said that?" she asked while looking at her sisters.

"Who said what?" replied Savannah.

Again, she heard her father's voice in an eerie, ghostly whisper. "Help! Olcnom. Oooolcnom!" With a look of fright on her face while holding the sword, she mumbled, "That! Who said Olcnom?"

A screech then sounded outside the cottage that startled all four girls. They all ran to the open door to see what had made such a despicable clatter. At first, some would mistake it as a dragon; they would indeed not be so lucky. Looking out into the thick blizzard, they beheld the most unusual fowl soaring down from the heavy pine treetops. The long, outstretched wings must have been 12 feet wide. With eyes as black as the night and feathers as dark as suffering anguish, the creature began to dart toward them with speed like a comet falling from the heavens. With outstretched talons that resembled daggers, the fowl exemplified no signs of goodwill toward them. The creature's sole purpose was to wage violence and inflict affliction.

"It's coming right toward us! Hurry! Shut the door!" Savannah screamed.

Scarlett then rushed toward the door and slammed it shut. Sophia ran to the table and took one of the wooden chairs and braced it against the broken door handle to hold it in place. The creature belted out another screech that began to fade away in the distant sky. A few seconds passed as they heard nothing except the snow falling outside and the pounding of their four hearts.

"What was that?" asked Savannah while clutching tightly to Sarah Honey. Sophia, still holding her father's sword, leaned against the door in a daze while looking at the kitchen table, almost lifeless.

"Sophia! Sophia!" shouted Scarlett. "What?" replied Sophia. Scarlett walked toward her and repeated, "I said, what was that?"

Sophia, still dazed, uttered what chillingly had been whispered in her ear by a voice like her father's. "Olcnom."

Scarlett threw her hands up in the air and said, "What are you talking about? Olcnom! What is that? What does that even mean?" She quietly shuffled away from the door and then to the fireplace.

"I . . . I heard Father whisper it to me right before that thing appeared," Sophia explained.

"Good grief, Sophia. You even said it yourself. Father is not here!" Scarlett shouted.

Confused as ever, Savannah, Scarlett, and Sarah Honey looked at Sophia, still trying to make sense of what had just taken place. With her heart still racing, Sophia lowered the sword to the floor—the same frozen floor they all stood barefoot on with toes obscured to the numbness of the cold. The horrific truth for the girls was that now they were numb to the reality in which they all resided—the harsh reality that . . . together . . . they were all alone.

Chapter Four

A Royal Army of Four

All their lives, their Mother and Father had given them direction and instruction. Their sweet, beautiful mother, Noel, had lectured them on manners and modesty. She spent many hours a day teaching the girls how to braid, sew, cook, and clean, and how a lady should conduct herself—even in the presence of the most crude and vile creature God ever created . . . man.

Speaking of the devil, Father had done his absolute best to prepare the girls for circumstances and hardships that he knew would eventually find them. He instilled in each of their hearts that there was nothing they were unable to accomplish, especially if they all stayed together. All four were taught the principles of pitching in, doing their part, and being there for one another in the trials of their young lives.

On each of the girls' sixth birthday, their father would place them on the family's largest horse, named Regal. Regal was a stout Clydesdale that consisted of nothing but pure muscle. He was practically part of the family. Father would spend many days plowing the field, dragging logs, and riding Regal through the woods. Mother was often annoyed due to Father's long conversations deep into the evening in the stable with his beloved horse.

There were no exceptions for the girls being scared or that Regal was too monstrous for them to mount. No choice or argument. They must overcome their fear and ride Regal. It was principles like these that the girls had experience in and were expected to overcome. The most important values that both Father and Mother had instilled in them were to stay rooted in God, never back down, and always stay together. That was exactly what Sophia knew they had to do. Stay together.

"What was that you said, Sophia? What does that mean?" asked Savannah as she held Sarah Honey by the hand. Sophia then walked away from the door and looked out the window. While trying to see if she could catch a glimpse of the horrifying creature that attempted to harm them, she replied, "I'm not sure, but we can't stay here. Whatever it was or whoever it was will be back. Maybe that is who took Mother and Father."

Sophia backed away from the window, appearing no longer as a young little girl but as a captain instructing an army of brave, fearless knights. "Girls, go get your bags that Mother knitted. Pack food and gather some water."

Scarlett walked toward Sophia with her hands up on her

head, fists full of her long brown hair, and shouted, "Pack! We can't leave while that thing is out there. Where are we going? What are you talking about?" Scarlett's face was now the color of a bloomed red rose, full of anger and frustration.

"Where are we going, Sophia?" quietly whispered Sarah Honey.

Sophia, the eldest of the four girls, began to make a decision her whole life had been preparing her for while she stood in the same spot her father had held the exact same sword near the fireplace. The question he had struggled with— "Can I wield the sword at my old age? Am I still capable?"—now his oldest daughter asked a similar question within herself. *Can I wield this sword at my young age? Am I capable?* Just as Father had reached for it when that devilish figure appeared, she too could waste no time debating if it could be done. Sophia knew it had to be done. The truth was that it had to be done if she wanted to find Mother and Father.

"I think we should stay here and wait for them to come home," Scarlett said with hands on her hips. "They probably just went out to get some firewood or out to the stable."

At that point, Sophia had heard enough. She slammed the cupboard door, turned with a stern look, and gave a furious order. "Listen! I am in charge. I'm the oldest, and that's that. I have helped take care of all of you your whole lives. Tonight is no different. From this point on, whatever I tell you to do, do it! No arguments! No suggestions! No opinions! Get your bags and fill them with some food and water. Now!"

All three of the girls' eyes lit up, and they suddenly gulped within their little throats with hands tucked behind their backs. They all began to go through the kitchen, searching for what food they could take along. A feeling of fear and nervousness filled their stomachs as they stuffed those hand-knitted bags Mother had made for them last Christmas with apples, oranges, carrots, potatoes, and a few stale biscuits Mother had made the previous morning for breakfast.

"Give me your water pouch, Sarah, and I'll fill it up." Savannah Gene was trying to assist and make sure everyone had something to drink for their unexpected journey. She was doing her best to provide for the girls just as Mother would have.

Sophia opened the cupboard where Mother kept her utensils and grabbed the three biggest knives. "Here. I want each of you to take one of these. I don't know how long we will be gone or even where exactly we're going, but I'd rather you have something to protect yourselves with."

Sarah Honey looked worried as if she were breaking an ultimate law or rule. "We're not supposed to play with these," she mumbled quietly.

"We're not playing, Sarah. Take it!" Sophia ordered.

Sarah hesitantly took the wooden-handled kitchen knife. Little did they know the blades were barely sharp enough to cut butter. Mother kept the sharp ones up high on the top shelf.

Once they all had packed their provisions and been issued dull butter knives, Sophia ordered, "Now go upstairs and get your heaviest quilts. Put on some extra stockings and be sure to dress warm." They all rushed up the stairs like a stampede of wild steer and obeyed what their oldest sister had instructed.

Without hesitation, the girls then frantically sprinted back down the stairs to await their next instructions. They all stood in a line, resembling brave soldiers during an inspection while serving in the Royal Golden Eagle Army. As Sophia walked by, she checked them carefully one by one. "Quilt, food, water, warm clothes, knife, and stockings. Okay. Next." She was cautious about walking out the door but certainly wanted to make sure that if they all had to go outside, they at least had to be prepared.

This army consisted of no calvary, no archers, no catapults, and not even a single flag to signify their coat of arms. They were just a small army of four girls under the age of eighteen with the purpose of finding and defending the ones they all loved.

Chapter Five

The Forbidden Black Ghost Forest

An incredible sight indeed, Sophia thought while looking at her three sisters. "Father would be proud," she said out loud, causing each of the girls to finally break the pressing frown painted on their little faces as they smiled. They all knew what they were about to try to do but within themselves questioned if they could even do it. They were all very young—Sophia was seventeen, Savannah fifteen, Scarlett thirteen, and Sarah Honey the sweet age of ten. Each girl was a reflection of their mother and father. Modesty and Integrity. Patience and Endurance. Gentleness and Power.

"Scarlett, button your cape and put on your . . ." Savannah mannerly and politely said.

"Uh . . . Fine!" Scarlett rolled her eyes and puffed as if she were a fire-breathing dragon. Sophia was also prepared, checking herself and making sure she, too, had packed all the necessities for their unknown journey. She then picked up her father's sword from the table. Standing there she could hardly keep it up with one hand due to its weight and sheer magnitude. Holding the sword up, she said, "When I open this door, we all stay together. Savannah, you go last. I want Scarlett and Sarah Honey in the middle. Understand?" All three nodded their heads and responded with a most undesirable and dreadful "Yes."

Unable to use a torch due to the drenched firewood covered in snow, the girls knew they were going out into the pitch-black darkness of night. The woods were known to be full of wolves, bears, and now whatever had paid them a visit earlier. Fright filled the room even more at the thought of enduring the frozen tundra and what continued to drift down from the sky. Sophia moved the chair and pulled the door open. A great gust of wind and snow blew right into their faces. If this were a sign of things to come, the journey was most certainly going to be full of hardships.

They had not yet even come face to face with whatever evil they knew resided beyond that front door. Just the freezing temperature and weather were enough to make even the fiercest warrior turn back and close the door. The howling wind cut into them and blew intensely, but they all knew this was it. The girls clung to their quilts and tucked themselves in tighter to embrace this already horrible challenge. As

Sophia took the first step through the door with her father's sword in hand, she accepted that there was no turning back now for the four of them.

As they shuffled out of the now-empty cottage, Sophia began to observe the area around her while also checking the trees above for the horrible, unwelcome intruder. Doing the best she could in the snow, her only help outside of her three sisters now appeared to be the brightly lit moon. It had begun to shine at its brightest in this hour of the night in which the snow-covered ground lit up to display a visible, unrecognizable trail.

"Look over there!" Sophia shouted, trying to overcome the noise of the tremendous, ghastly wind as it combed through their long, damp hair. With each of them struggling to catch a glimpse of the sight, she said aloud, "Follow me and stay together!" Pushing their way through the deep snow, they could now see the tracks their oldest sister had pointed out. The tracks resembled a large object being drug through the caked, frozen ground from their cottage and straight to the woods. "Come on! Maybe that's where Mother and Father are!" Sophia shouted.

They all shuffled and continued into the woods, trying their best to stay close together. The heavy snow began to dwindle a bit due to the thickness of the trees while inside the wooded area. The girls were somewhat familiar with these woods, but the farther they pushed through, the more fearful they became. They continued with the moon and trail as their only guides.

Savannah shouted to Sophia, "I think this is far enough!"

Sophia, showing no signs of being deterred, responded, "No the trail keeps going. Come on!"

Savannah yelled back, "Sophia, you do know where this is leading us, don't you?"

Scarlett turned back and gave a fearful look at Savannah, finally showing that she, too, had the ability to be somewhat afraid. The large, peculiar trail then led them straight from the woods to the forest. This was not just any forest. It was the haunted Black Ghost Forest.

Never were they allowed to step foot inside this forbidden place all these years. Curiosity, though, always solicited their minds, wondering what could possibly lay beyond the entrance to such a spooky, grim place. What danger roamed about inside its thick wooded walls? Were the tales true about its name? Was there an actual ghost clothed in a black cloak that truly haunted it? What other reasons may be concealed within it? Mother and Father never gave the exact reason why the girls were forbidden to enter, but they would just say, "No matter what, do not go into the Black Ghost Forest."

The girls were all in disbelief as they stood there shivering, huddled together and contemplating whether to take the first step into this awful place or turn back. The mysterious trail did not turn east, west, or most certainly not south back to their now-empty cottage. Straight ahead and north was the direction that now may lead them to their beloved parents.

"Sophia, we can't go in there! Mother and Father forbade it!" Savannah said with a teeth-chattering plea.

As the snow continued to land on her already wet, brown hair, Sophia gazed deep within the heart of that forest. Black, empty and desolate it was. After all these years of being warned about the present danger, why would they enter this haunted forest now? The words her father used to justify the deeds of warfare he had committed in his mind now entered his eldest daughter's consciousness. "It must be done," repeatedly echoed in her soul.

"We have no choice, Savannah!" Sophia shouted. She then retrieved her father's sword from the small leather sheath looped within her belt. With the hilt desperately and firmly clutched in her hands, north she went, holding the sword as if charging into battle. The little army must now be prepared to endure whatever evil dwelled within the Black Ghost Forest.

Chapter Six

A Tale No One Would Believe

Chilling and eerie were the feelings all four girls experienced as they cautiously tiptoed through the forsaken, haunted forest. Occasions such as this compared to walking into a freshly spindled spider web or the sound of wolves howling nearby as the sun descends while picking berries. This undeniable unpleasant emotion placed a blanket of fear over them all. It appeared that the darkness had increased upon entering this forest as the heavy snowfall seemed to cease from the crowded thickness of the monstrous, gigantic trees.

Now that their vision became somewhat clearer to see a stone cast in front of them, they all had now felt the bitter cold of reality. They were now within the mercy of the Black Ghost Forest. With each step, a shiver crawled up their spines like a hideous rat with the sudden snap of a twig or bending of a snow-covered limb. Their eyes mocked them as every shadow cast by the moonlight seemed to be a grisly monster or moaning ghost. Pitches of laughter in the distance and nearby rang in their ears as they all became spooked and fearful. "What was that?" whispered Scarlett. Each of them, afraid to make a peep, stood there frozen from the terror and the harsh, unmerciful cold.

Scanning the area, they continued following the trail. The farther they went, Sophia noticed the wide, gaping snow trail begin to fade. She was troubled within herself at the uncertainty that the trail would even lead them to their dear mother and father. She continuously heard the word softly whispered in her ear, "Olcnom." What could it mean? Surely this had to be a sign, a clue, or a plea in the attempt to locate them. Not as a mere coincidence, Sophia truly felt that somehow her father was trying to tell her something. At this point, nothing seemed impossible. She knew it was not the tricks of the forest since it was in the cottage she had first become familiar with the word, the place, or the thing. That was the confusing and conflicting struggle that she wrestled with each step in that cursed forest.

Even though the terrain was much denser than any woods they had experienced, this did not deter them from continuing to cut through the thick forest with precision. With each stride, they held desperately to the desire to be as quiet as they possibly could.

Unbeknownst to them, they had already accomplished

far more than what even the most daring soul would do in the Righteous Kingdom. Many brutes would often boast in the smoky, grimy taverns while filling their bellies with freshly roasted mutton and each other's ears with tall tales long enough to reach the tops of a beanstalk. They exaggerated late into the night with stretched accounts of slaying dragons, pulling the feather from a sleeping griffin, or even the ability to have whipped one of the fabled giants. The girls had never seen any of those but had only been entertained by their father with similar bedtime stories. He would often raise his hand at the end of each one and say, "I promise. It 'tis true. I give you my word."

None, though, would even dare utter the phrase that they had entered the Black Ghost Forest. Such negative and profane statements had never echoed in those dusty tavern walls within the Kingdom. If they had, that brave soul would refuse to mention the effect it had on their poor mind. Amazingly and oddly enough, these four girls were not only in the Black Ghost Forest, but in the forest at the witching hour.

Suddenly there was a loud shriek from high above the trees. It was the same horrific sound of that fowl beast they witnessed back at the cottage hours ago. Gazing above, they could see that mammoth creature soar above their heads. "Quick! Hide! Over there!" whispered Sophia. The girls frantically ran over and burrowed themselves underneath several fallen logs for cover, praying that they weren't seen and holding as still as possible. Just as a vulture circles its prey, so too was this demon in the sky.

"Is it gone?" asked Sarah Honey. "Ssshhhhh." Sophia held her finger over her lips. They could hear the creature's large wings flapping and cutting through the windy sky. A large feather fell and landed in front of Scarlett's face. Her eyes lit up, resembling the bright moon due to its immense size. How scary to think that you were the one being hunted. But hunted by what? What could this creature be?

Several minutes passed, each second feeling like an hour. Sophia then peeked her head out from under the log. In the distance she saw the creature fly away as it gave one last shrilling shriek into the lonesome night sky. "I think it's gone," she said. A look and feeling of joy filled all of them, but each knew this was not the last they would encounter this beast. The Black Ghost would not give up that easily.

The girls slowly crept out from underneath the logs and shook off the compacted snow and dirt that clung to their quilts. They now began to finally feel the full effect of this harsh, winter storm. With all the hardships the girls had already endured, it seemed they were now going to catch somewhat of a break. The heavy snow had apparently stopped, and as luck would have it, night had begun to give way to dawn.

One would consider that in the forest there are often consistent and pleasant events upon the breaking of dawn—the lovely singing of a gleeful robin, the tweeting of graceful sparrows, and even the sight of a scampering, bushy, gray squirrel rushing down an acorn tree to start its daily harvest. Not here. Not in the Black Ghost Forest. No singing.

No chirping. No tweeting. No signs of joyful life. One word could be used to describe its habitat and surroundings—dead. All good things appear to have been forsaken in this place many years ago. Even the magnificent sun rising over the mountain and trees with its powerful rays could not produce even the slightest shade of color. All seemed to be held to the pigment of either pale or gray.

But why? Sophia thought while she continued to carefully survey the landscape. After it is all said and done, each girl would agree that this night would be considered the longest of their lives. Each girl now had a tale to brag about back home, but they knew within themselves that nobody would dare believe what they had already accomplished together. Together—all alone in the Black Ghost Forest.

Chapter Seven

The Road to Nowhere

There were two things that filled the girls' hearts with joy as they continued to hike in such a dreadful place—the bright sunshine and the quick melting of the snow. They were tired, exhausted, and cold as their little noses ran profusely with each inhale. If it had not been for the warmth of the sun, they no doubt would have flirted with icicles hanging about their faces in due time. The bright yellow rays of the sun had pierced through the thick, snow-covered treetops and made their way to the white-laden ground.

"Oh no! The trail is melting! Its disappearing!" Sophia shouted. The snowy trail began to turn into a messy, muddy ditch. The only clue that was possibly leading them to their beloved mother and father was fading quickly. Sophia jumped up and rushed toward the depleting trail, kicking up piles of snow behind her.

"I have to stop for a minute, Sophia. I'm hungry, and my feet hurt," Scarlett said as she collapsed on top of a fallen tree perched on the ground.

"We can't stop, Scarlett. The trail is disappearing!" Sophia called back. "This is the only clue we have that may lead us to where Mother and Father are, and you want to fill your mouth with food?" Sophia paced back and forth in front of the other three girls. The eldest of the four had forgotten that her sisters were only young, innocent girls—not experienced soldiers.

"Sophia, they need to rest for a minute," Savannah argued. "We have been following this trail all night, and it has not led us anywhere but deep into this haunted forest. We need to rest for a moment!" Savannah Gene, who rarely loses her temper, had begun to feel the toll that the cold, the hunger, and the journey were already taking.

"Fine! But you had better eat it quickly!" Sophia sternly instructed.

Savannah graciously walked over to Sarah Honey and tucked her quilt in to keep her little body warm. She picked the leaves and branches out of her cinnamon braided hair, just as Mother would have done if she were there.

While sitting atop the fallen tree, Sarah Honey began to whimper and cry. Savannah wrapped her arms around her and held her tight. "Oh, it's okay. Everything will be alright. Don't you worry." At that very moment, something happened that had never occurred in this terrible place. Kindness. Love was exemplified and displayed, cracking the stony grim heart of the Black Ghost Forest.

They all began pulling the food they had packed out of their bags with excitement just as one would imagine good old Saint Nick would do as he retrieved those sought-after presents. With each bite of a frozen orange or a dry stale biscuit, they all dug in to nullify the pain of hunger. As Scarlett lifted her water pouch for a drink to wash down the dry biscuit, she realized nothing was coming out. She began to shake the pouch and discovered that it had frozen completely. "It's frozen!" she shouted as her face began to fuel red.

"Here, Scarlett, you can have some of mine." Sarah Honey graciously handed her the ice-filled water pouch.

The eerie feeling began to loosen its grip on the four after traveling through the haunted forest all night into morning. With the comfort that thankfully grew while they explored the habitat they were in, they were still unaware of the effects the wicked forest was having on them. Strife and war were brewing like a potion in a black, steaming cauldron between the four sisters as they all questioned each decision they had made inside their wandering minds. Each knew in their hearts that none desired to be there. In all honesty, though, no one would. With all the mystery that encompassed them, the most challenging of all rang in their minds. What happened to Mother and Father? How did they just vanish? What explanation could be given for a circumstance that all four could not comprehend? As an untraveled road wanders, so too does one's thoughts in uncertainty.

"Alright, let's go." Sophia said as she finished her last ice-covered orange slice. While quickly stuffing their mouths, they all put their hoods on and tightly wrapped their quilts around them. Onward they went, partaking in an expedition with no recollection where it would lead them.

Farther they pressed as the snow trail they had been using for a guide began to disappear, just as their poor mother and father had. As the day went on, the sun again appeared to be on their side. The temperature had increased, although the harsh winter chill fought to resume its rightful place.

After a steady stroll through the forest, Sophia abruptly halted, causing the girls one by one to bump into each other. She frantically looked at the ground. Turning as a hunting dog that had lost the guiding scent of the trail, she barked, "It's gone! The trail! It's completely gone!" She turned and looked at Savannah with a defeated expression. "What do we do now?"

Scarlett mumbled while shivering uncontrollably beside Sarah Honey. With the nightmare of being lost in the Black Ghost Forest, she also came to realize their chances of finding their parents decreased dramatically if any chance had remained at all. The road that possibly led to them had now vanished.

Life had appeared from the trees as several large crows, dark as coal, sat atop the branches with their eyes fixated on the halted crusade. "Listen. What's that noise?" Savannah asked. They all paused and remained still.

"It sounds like water," Sarah quietly responded. They could hear the sound of running water close by.

"Follow me," Sophia whispered as the line began to move once again. The roar of the river grew louder as they approached. A thick bushel of thorns and thistles hindered them from uncovering the enticing sound. "Stand back," Sophia said as she withdrew her father's sword from her belt. Unable to hide the weight and magnitude of the sword, she swung violently down into the brush. She let out an awful grunt as the girls watched from behind her, out of the way.

"Is it too heavy for ya?" Scarlett mischievously muttered.

Sophia gave her a look of frustration and warning as she raised it above her head once more. After several blows to the barricade, Sophia had now cut a path through the thicket. As they stepped over the brush, they noticed a crushing waterfall upstream that must have been 15 feet high. Frozen icicles draped over the falls that appeared to the eye to be larger than old Regal.

Below where they gazed, the water was calmer, not flowing as swiftly but looked to be very deep. Just as luck would have it, the crossing seemed too wide with depths as deep as a dark, gloomy pit.

"Down there! Look! We can go across that tree!" Sophia shouted, trying to overcome the roar and continuous pound of the waterfall.

As they followed Sophia, Scarlett spoke up. "I don't . . . think this is a good idea."

Kicking the fallen tree, Sophia quickly turned around and said, "Do you have a better idea? If so, tell me! Let's hear it! Please! What do you think we should do?"

Savannah and Sarah both looked down toward the ground without either saying a word or making a sound.

Scarlett scanned the area, searching for another option, idea, or choice rather than crossing over the top of the dreadful, deep-freezing river. With no argument or suggestion to present, Scarlett stood there silently.

"That's what I thought," Sophia proclaimed. "Stay here. I'll go across first to see if it's safe." Sophia then jumped on top of the snow-covered tree, lost her footing, slipped, and fell flat on her back.

"Oh my! Are you okay, Sophia?" Savannah yelled while she and Sarah ran over. The two began to dust the snow and mud off their sister while attempting to assist her back to her feet. Scarlett then leaned back and belted out in laughter while pointing. "Hahahahaha! Oh yes! Great idea, Captain!"

All the girls knew their oldest sister was not exactly considered the most graceful and poised of the four. Clumsy is a word that comes to mind that one would most certainly use to describe her. Sophia then regained her composure as she carefully stepped back up onto the fallen tree. Once again, just as Father had put her back on top of Regal as a little girl, she knew that giving up was not an option. Those life lessons Father had instilled in her had paid off after all these years. As prideful as she was, though, it did appear that the road she was leading her sisters on felt like . . . a road to nowhere.

Chapter Eight

Help from High Above

The sharp breeze of the wind coming from the rushing waterfall kissed Sophia's face as she proceeded to cross to the other side. Nose dripping, eyes watering, and hands numb, she felt as if it could not possibly get worse. Several of the pesky crows began cawing above as they darted straight toward her down from the sky.

"Watch out!" Savannah screamed as three of the menacing birds flew around her head as if trying to prevent her from crossing.

Sophia's heart sank as her snow-caked foot slipped from the makeshift bridge. Time felt as if it had slowed down as she fell backward. Her eyes now open wide in distress, she could see the rays of sunshine piercing through the clouds as they overshadowed the fowl that started to circle her. Splash! The perpetual shock then flowed through her veins as icy temperatures consumed her whole body. The sudden hysterical screams of her three poor sisters translated into nothing but a mumbling blur.

As Sophia struggled to reach the surface, she felt as though something had tangled itself around her foot. She looked down to see what was preventing her from escaping the icy river. Looking down, she saw that it was not weeds or brush, and she was not ledged between a rock that laid hold of her foot. What hindered her was nothing of the ordinary but of the unordinary. It was a skeleton! A skeleton with life!

Sophia's eyes flashed brightly as her mouth opened wide, screaming in disbelief and causing bubbles to instantly float to the top. The skeleton, with its chilling clutch of death upon her foot, began to climb up her leg—and it was not alone. Two more appeared from beneath the thick riverbed as they surrounded her from behind. As they laid hold of her, she began to fight and kick the best she could, but it seemed to cause them no harm.

The quilt her beloved mother had sewn for her as a gift on her tenth birthday now sank helplessly to the dark, muddy depths, and she could only watch. Her vision became dim, and her sisters' screams began to fade as they desperately watched. While the skeletons continued to drag her down, another one appeared and began to pry her father's sword from her belt. These few seconds trapped within the river graveyard felt as if it were an eternity. Sophia vigorously fought while clinging to her dear father's sword. She refused to bestow the creatures the honor to possess what he had held so dear to his heart. After all, it could be all she had left of him. Hopeless and alone she felt while struggling within the river's deep.

A bright light began to appear in her beautiful blue eyes while thoughts raced within her mind—memories of wrestling with Father in the wheat fields, cooking with Mother, and playing with dolls with her sisters. It was true, she thought. Life really does pass before your eyes during these last mortal moments. With no more strength left inside of her, she begrudgingly accepted her fate.

Just as she thought her life had come to an end at the young age of seventeen, she felt something grab the hood of her cloak. A powerful rush as strong as the waterfall pulled her from the depths of the river and brought her straight to the surface. Momentarily she felt as if her soul had left her body and was finally on her path to heaven. Splat! Sophia landed hard on the frozen ground on the other side of the river. She realized that somehow she had escaped the cold clutch of death.

Cough! Cough! Cough! While rolling over to gather her breath and consciousness, Sophia could now see that somehow her sisters were also on the same side of the river. Confused by how they had crossed so safely, she began to look around the ground for her father's sword. While gazing about, she noticed something that was not so familiar. She saw a set of feet right in front of her. They were much larger than any feet she had ever seen.

At first, she had mistaken them for two tree trunks hewn down by a local beaver, but as one of them moved, she knew that was not so. The thick, stocky feet resembled the feet of a bear. "BBBBBear!" she tried to scream, but her teeth were chattering as ice began to form about her soaked and nearly frozen hair and face. No doubt this animal—creature, thing—was larger than anything she had ever seen. As she quickly gazed up, she knew that her next sight would be a mouth open wide, full of razor-sharp teeth and prepared to enjoy a midday snack.

As the cold water dripped from her nose, Sophia began to get up on her knees. The figure that towered over her appeared to be as tall as the ceiling in their cottage and as wide as the fireplace mantel. To her surprise, it was not an animal, creature, or bear—but a giant! Looking up, she could see a long, brown beard with streaks of gray drooping down his rough, round, dirty face to his large, oversized belly. Patches of hair covered his Christmas-goose-sized hands sticking out from his torn, raggedy top constructed of sewn bear hide. On his shoulders were paws sewn in with the claws draping down, giving him a menacing appearance. The giant also had the longest pair of stitched britches made of red flannel that she had ever seen. It was an intimidating and gut-churning sight. He was a brute with large, stout arms and legs as thick as a cow's head.

"Are ya alright, love?" asked her monstrous savior with a thunderous yet gentle, raspy, Gaelic voice. He stood there with both hands placed on his hips, gazing down from what appeared to be the heavens. Confused and still trying to collect her thoughts, Sophia turned and looked at her three sisters while they stood calmly behind her rescuer. "I'm dreaming," Sophia said aloud.

"Nope. Not a dream, me lit'l angel," the giant uttered.

Could it be so? she thought while still looking up from the ground. After all, Father always said nothing is impossible, and now before her stood a true, living, breathing giant!

The gargantuan man wiped his large nose just as a child with a cold and inquired again, "Are ya alright, lass?" Sophia frantically tried to stand to her feet as quickly as she could, but with her body still frozen, she stumbled back to the ground. "Here now. Let me give ya a help'n hand," the giant said while walking toward her.

Frightened, Sophia then sprang up, pulled her father's sword from her soaked leather belt, and shouted, "Halt, beast! That's close enough!" With the end of the chipped sword now poking the behemoth's round belly, Sophia's arms began to shake as she shivered with each breath.

The giant suddenly stopped and swiftly threw his arms up in the air as though he had been caught committing a distasteful crime. "Sophia, it's okay. Stop!" shouted Savannah. She walked toward the two and put her hand on Sophia's hand that gripped the golden handle of the iron sword. "He helped us across the river and is the one who pulled you out."

Sophia looked at her sisters, turned toward the river, and examined the water graveyard but for a moment. She then lowered the sword slowly and cautiously to the ground.

"Shewww," the giant spewed with his eyes opened as large as fresh eggs from the coup. He dropped his hands down to his sides and took a deep sigh of relief. "Those pesky lit'l Creatlaches 'bout got the best of ya, aye love?" he said with a devilish grin.

"Creatlaches?" Sophia nervously said, still shivering underneath her wet clothes.

"Those are the Beo Creatlaches—living skeletons that lurk within the forest," the giant explained. "Evil and nasty those lit'l bug . . ." He then turned and looked back at little Sarah Honey, thankful he had held his tongue. Choosing not to corrupt her poor, innocent ears, he turned back to Sophia and mannerly continued. "Um . . . those lit'l devils. They are ruthless. I can't even go berry pick'n without 'em try'n ta gut me with a pok'a." With all the circumstances, the giant then became aware that he had not told them who he was. "Oh, stall the ball! I'm sorry! I haven't properly introduced myself." He then placed his left hand over his heart in the most courteous way and extended his right hand out while bending down. "I'm Ybbub. And ye might be?"

Sophia again glanced back at her sisters as they all stood there with smiles while behind him. Lifting her hand, she placed it in the rough, calloused pit that the giant called his hand. Gently he shook her hand as she became more comfortable with the reality that she was now standing in the presence of a giant.

"I'm . . . Sophia." Pointing behind him, she said, "Those are my sisters. That's Sav . . ."

Ybbub interrupted, holding both hands up, gesturing her to stop. "No! No! No! Wait! Let me guess their names."

One by one he turned and pointed at each of the three girls. Starting with Savannah, he went down the line. "You must be Pennywinkle. And uh, you—you must be Tweedle." He stared at Sarah Honey, examining her with both arms crossed about his chest and then tapping his finger about his bearded chin. "Hmmmm. And that makes you . . . Walnuts!" Ybbub began clapping his hands in excitement as if he had guessed a thousand-year-old riddle with a smile that must have been a foot wide.

The girls all snickered and giggled but would not dare discourage the gleeful giant while he celebrated. Sophia then corrected him. "Uh no. I'm sorry. That's Savannah, that's Scarlett, and that's Sarah—Sarah Honey."

Ybbub paused his clapping and ceased his earthquaking jig. He responded, all the while trying to hide the disappointment about his face. "Oh well. I was close, though, wasn't I?" Ybbub tried to hide his disappointment and embarrassment. He then patted Sophia atop her cold, wet head and said, "Never mind that. Now that we've introduced ourselves, I'm sure you lit'l lasses are plum knackered. Let's get a fire built, and we'll warm ya up a bit."

Chapter Nine

A Giant Plea

The warm, crackling fire was worth more to the freezing little girls than Ybbub's weight in solid gold. They all huddled together as Sophia sat next to Savannah; hands extended trying to thaw her fingers while sharing the quilt. Walking to the fire, Ybbub threw several more logs on top as sparks flew into the evening sky, and then he sat down. "That'll do," he mumbled, swatting the mud and dirt from his oversized hands.

An awkward silence filled the air, and only burning wood could be heard among them. The giant then leaned to his left side and raised his tree-sized leg. A horrendous wail echoed, and an even worse distasteful smell filled the unoccupied void. "Apologies, my lit'l angels. Dearly. Apologies. Too many blueberries I tell ya."

The girls all held their noses and burrowed their faces into the quilts for some form of relief. "Good grief!" yelled

Scarlett as she attempted to fan away the disgusting stench that now surrounded her.

"I said I was sorry. What?" he whispered in his defense while holding his head down toward the ground in shame.

As Sophia sat there, the glow of the flames flashed on the hilt of the sword and caught Ybbub's eye. "Where did ya get that dragon pok'a?" he curiously asked. "It's a dandy now, that 'tis." Sophia steadily tucked the sword back under the quilt that she and Savannah were sharing. "Ya nearly gutted me, ya know. If ya ain't careful, you'll cut ya bloom'n fingers off . . . like I did!" He held up his large hand, palm facing him as he slyly held down two of his fingers, making it appear like he only had three on the one hand. Sarah Honey's mouth opened wide in amazement as the girls were instantly pulled into his playful ruse. Ybbub let out a sneeze, finally releasing the other two fingers. A boisterous laugh then belted deep from his belly. Sarah and Savannah started clapping their hands as if watching a wizard perform at his best. Sophia remained quiet, still refusing to acknowledge his question in reference to the sword.

Ybbub scooted closer to the warm, beaming fire and went on to his next inquiry. "Now then. If ya don't mind me ask'n, what are four lit'l lasses doin' deep within the Black Ghost Forest?" They all remained silent as each looked to Sophia like soldiers at their commanding officer. "Come now. What's ye purpose here?"

Sophia questioned if she could truly trust this mammoth giant that they had only met several hours earlier. Who was he? Where did he come from? Could he have taken Mother and Father? After considering each aspect of their interaction, she thought that if he honestly had immoral intentions, why would he have saved her from the Beo Creatlaches?

Before Sophia could open her mouth, Scarlett sprang out from her warm quilt and shouted, "You tell us! Don't act like you don't know! We've been following your trail all night, and it led us straight to your big old . . ."

Savannah jumped up from the ground and rushed to her sister. "Stop, Scarlett! That's enough."

Scarlett raised her right fist up to Ybbub's nose as he sat there. Shaking her fist with knuckles clinched, she proceeded to shout, "Now I've stayed quiet long enough! Where are they? Where's Mother and Father?"

Ybbub once again held his hands up in an innocent, pleading act as his eyes crossed carefully, fixated on Scarlett's tightly balled fist before his large, bumpy nose. The fearful, burly giant frantically gulped as those in attendance watched to see what would happen next. Indeed it 'twas a match for the ages as a 5½-foot thirteen-year-old girl stood before an 8-foot quisby behemoth. As you might have guessed, the odds were no doubt in Scarlett's favor.

"Now wait just a bloom'n minute," the giant said while nervously trembling. "I don't gotta hinker'n of what you're even talk'n about!" While watching the legendary clash of the two irresistible forces, Sarah Honey pulled out a biscuit from her satchel and captivatingly ate while enjoying the show.

"Honestly, I ain't got the slightest id . . ." Ybbub paused

mid-sentence as he began to sniff like a prized hunting dog. His attention was no longer entertained by the potential threat that stood before him, but now he was unquestionably intrigued by the favoring scent that lingered in his presence. He began crawling on all fours with his snozzle high in the air, attempting to track down the wonderful, buttery, flaky scent. "Do I . . . do I smell . . ." Ybbub sniffed deeply while he held his nose high in the air. The skillful giant followed the scent while crawling about the ground on his hands and knees. The buttery aroma led him directly to little Sarah Honey who sat there quietly eating her treat. The youngest of the four looked up and beheld the giant, stuck in a mesmerized state.

"Do I smell biscuits?" Ybbub's mouth began to water as he closed his eyes and licked his large, cracked lips. Rubbing his hands together, he politely asked, "Would you be so kind as to maybe give me a lit'l pinch? It looks awful scrumptious. I mean . . . you're not gonna eat all of that, are ya?"

Sarah kindly reached down into her knitted bag and retrieved another biscuit. With the dry, stony snack held in her tiny, smooth hand, she raised it up to Ybbub. He swiftly grabbed the biscuit from her hand and gobbled it up in one bite. "Oh my," he said while chewing and smacking his lips in the most unpleasant way. "Now that's a great treat for the ol' belly." Sticking his hand up toward his face, he began licking the crumbs on his fingers. Scarlett gave a look of disapproval and curled her lip as his mannerisms churned her belly.

Sarah then stood up and spoke. "Can you help us? Help us find our mother and father? We don't know where they are. Will you please help us?"

Looking around, Ybbub beheld the desperation beset upon all four of the little girls' faces—too young to conceal emotion and, just as a child, not too prideful to ask for help. "I . . . I don't . . . I don't know," he reluctantly mumbled.

Savannah quickly grabbed her satchel and removed all the biscuits, oranges, and morsels of food that remained inside. "Here! Take it all. Take it. Please, Ybbub. We need your help," Savannah pled, offering to sacrifice all she had to find her dear parents. The fearsome, reckless giant of the Black Ghost Forest smiled as he looked down at Savannah Gene. His watermelon-sized heart began to melt while viewing the desperation trapped within her beautiful hazel eyes.

Ybbub gently pushed aside the sweet child's offering with a choked-up voice and mumbled, "I . . . I don't know where they are."

Scarlett's face became painted red, filled with rage. She shouted, "Liar! I don't believe you!"

They all stood to their feet and gathered next to Scarlett as Sophia spoke. "We need your help. We must find them. Please, Ybbub. Please."

The giant scratched the top of his balding head, rubbed the back of his grimy neck, and then anxiously took a bite from the apple he had picked up from the ground. With a mouthful of apple, he said, "I don't know where they are, but I might know someone who does."

Chapter Ten

Shredded by the Wheat

"Stay close now. Try to keep up," Ybbub whispered while motioning with his hand as the girls continued to follow from behind. The eerie forest regained its unequivocal hold as thoughts imitated spiders crawling up their backs and into their minds. Scattered fog had set in, making the journey more difficult to pass through while in the unfamiliar terrain. The bright, warm hug of the sunlight they all had joyfully basked in earlier had been choked lifeless by the thickness of an uncontrollable cloud. Suddenly the sound of strange fowls echoed in the distance high above. Being unable to see caused the girls even more fear and anxiety in the heart of this haunted forest.

Even while in the company of a bearskin-clothed, 8 foot giant, they all bore the dreadful weight and hindrance of fear. A snowy trail had led them from their cottage into the Black Ghost Forest. Now the only sense of direction they depended on was the questionable memory of a newly acquainted giant. With every step, the girls prayed Ybbub was certain that the path he was leading them on was the right path indeed. When one follows the lead of another, the destination is only truly known to the one who's leading.

Thoughts of Mother and Father sternly warning them daily about this terrible place resonated in their minds. Ten years ago, Sophia heard her father speak about the desolate forest to one of his close friends while shoeing Regal at the stable in the spring. Her father was unaware that she was collecting eggs. She hid behind the coop as her father continued his conversation. She overheard him mention a little girl who had run away from the Righteous Kingdom and was last seen stepping into the Black Ghost Forest. It occurred several years before any of the four girls were born. He told how many men were sent into the forest to find her, but only a few returned. Supposedly, the little girl's mother and father never returned either. An entire family was lost and consumed by the evil that resided in the Black Ghost Forest. The little girl and her family were never found or seen again.

Will we return? Sophia thought. As they creeped through the forest, Scarlett began asking Ybbub questions that had been weighing on her mind since the moment they had met.

"Do you really eat people?" Sophia asked.

Ybbub looked down and quickly replied, "What? Eat a bloom'n human?"

Scarlett looked and studied the giant as he continued to claim his innocence.

"No. No. No," the giant went on. "Ya got me confused with me uncle Etin. Well, my uncles to be exact. Ol' fella's got three heads. Manky he is, but quite craic, I'll give'em that. From the other side of the old homeland. Skipped over the blue waters to a darker shamrock let's say. Aye! Now Uncle Etin does eat . . . I mean did, uh, eat people."

The curious little girl continued her interrogation while following his lead, "Do you really pick the meat out of your teeth with the leg bone of a griffin?"

Shocked, Ybbub said, "Whaaaa? A . . . the leg bone of a griffin? You're quite the melter, aren't ya? A wooden pale of annoyance you are! Do you know that?"

Savannah quickly interjected, "Mice—I've heard giants are deathly afraid of mice."

Ybbub's bear-skin boots froze instantly in his tracks. He turned around and began nodding his large, round head and wagging his finger. "Aye. Aye. Now that's true. Why? Do ya see one?"

Sarah Honey giggled as she noticed the necklace that swayed about his chest. "What's that claw, Ybbub?"

The giant saw the twinkle in her little blue eyes as she adored its unique appearance. "Ya like that, do ya?" he asked with a wide grin peeking through his rough, dirty beard. "That there . . . is a griffin's claw. Don't go ask'n how I got it. Believe you me, that's what it is. No one would dare believe me anyway." The tender giant then lifted the tethered necklace from about his large noggin and put it over Sarah's head. "It's yours now, ya lit'l angel." A playful raspy laugh came from his jolly soul. "No one will believe where ya got it from!"

Ybbub found himself truly beginning to feel relaxed while in the presence of unusual company in such an unusual place. Always bearing the trouble of being alone in the most dreadful habitat does make one question each interaction they have. His whole life had been spent being on guard, brawling, and always having to deal with the worst side of people. "Ya know, it's nice to be in the company of such lovely duines."

Savannah scrunched her brow and asked, "Duines? What's a duine?"

Ybbub laughed, "You, me lit'l lass. A regular folk. A duine!" He chuckled under his breath and mumbled, "Usually they run away or hide before I can get the first bite." Scarlett turned back to Savannah and gave her a look of fright.

After walking through the foggy forest for about three hours, the group suddenly came to a halt. Ybbub placed his finger to his chin and began to tap as he thought aloud. "Hmm . . . Let me see here." Turning around looking up to the trees, he squinted his egg-sized eyes and slowly walked toward an old oak tree. Taking his fist, the giant then knocked four times as if checking the ripeness of a melon.

He released a jubilant shout while tapping his noggin. "That way, lit'l angels. I knew I was right. I knew it! Oh, we'll have a whale of a time now, that we will. Come on! This way." With no other choice, they all followed the giant as if they were chicks following their mother hen.

The thickness of the trees now began to spread abroad, allowing a somewhat more visible view of their path. Wide and large vegetation inhabited this certain part of the Black Ghost Forest. They were much taller and wider than any they had ever seen. The tops clearly appeared as brushes painting the stars in the coolness of night while bending in the wind.

While Sophia gazed upon their greatness and magnitude, she noticed they somewhat resembled the trees people in the village often spoke about—gigantic, massive trees that can move, walk, and even . . . talk—voices so deafening they are often mistaken for clashes of thunder. They were known among the folk as Stagnus Trees. She whispered, turning to Savannah, "Do you really think?" Savannah continued her gaze while mesmerized by their majestic and mythical proportion.

"A blessin' from the heavens above! We found it." Ybbub proudly placed his hands on his hips and tapped his bear-hide feet in a swift jig. He winked at Sarah Honey while she observed the joyous celebration. "I just hope they're home," he nervously said.

"Hope!" Scarlett responded in frustration. "Wait right here."

Ybbub walked past the tree line where the girls all stood and tiptoed toward the small cottage. "Looks like a witch lives here," Scarlett said, looking around the open area. The small cottage was made of stone and lovingly complemented by a thick, snug, straw roof. Ybbub saw a wooden pen and smelled to the right of the cottage where several hogs were frantically rolling and squealing about. A sturdy wooden door sat at the center. Two secured windows with matching wooden shutters displayed a somewhat inviting but cautious message. To the left was a stone well for drawing water that indeed appealed to be very tempting to indulge in.

Ybbub tiptoed to the cottage like a cat sneaking upon a robin and put his ear against the wooden door and listened. After several seconds, he gently knocked three times. Knock! Knock! Knock! When there was no response, he whispered, "Augustus, you in there?" The girls anxiously waited for a response, a sound, or a joyful invitation. But they heard, "Who wants ta know?" A woman's voice came from inside.

Ybbub began shaking his head in disappointment while placing his hands in his face as if he had just made a terrible mistake. "Umm . . . it's me! It's ya dear ol' Ybbub. Is Augustus home?" There was the clang of numerous locks and bolts like those of a great castle, and the door briskly swung open.

"Tootie!" yelled Ybbub with his arms stretched out, offering a cheerful greeting for an invited embrace. An old woman bearing an affectionate smile and not appearing yet sixty-one was standing in the doorway in front of the giant. She wore a kerchief about her head that kept the not-so-tidy gray hair from her face, and a shabby white-and-yellow dress. Around her waist was a dark red apron covered with stains and baking flour, which painted the picture of a well-self-taught baker. What was believed to be a sweet meeting of two friendly acquaintances turned out to be nothing of the sort.

As Ybbub stood there patiently waiting to receive her warm embrace, the old woman slowly changed her expression. The old lady slammed the door in his face. Ybbub continued to stand there motionless. “Tootie! Please!”

The old woman swung the door back open, releasing a violent tirade that the girls had never seen before or since. “Why you no good, smell-feast, pie-stealing, quisby son of a turnip!”

Ybbub held his hands up again in a peaceful manner while crying in defense. “Now . . . uh . . . wait, Tootie!”

Fire filled the old woman’s eyes as she continued to use slander unfit for a grown man’s ears. “Don’t you sweet Tootie me! How dare you show your face here, you mammoth mountain goat, pig tail, sack of haggis waste!”

Ybbub started to back away from the door as he continued to pour salt into his own wound. “Tootie if this is about the pie, I’m sorry.”

The old woman screamed and darted frantically back inside. Instantly an arsenal of kettles, pots, and pans began flying from the cottage and out the door. It was as if a commander had signaled for catapults to be launched toward the opposing pressing army. She was swift and, dare I say, accurate. The giant turned away as a child being chased by a buzzing swarm of determined honeybees.

“Ouch! Now listen here, uh, wait, Tootie! Ouch! That’s enough now!” One after another she beaned the giant with great precision while showing no sign of a retreat of volley. Still to this day, it 'tis a marvelous thought to wonder how much cookware was kept inside such a small stony cottage.

Finally, the hailstorm of cast iron ceased. The girls watched by the wood line as they stood still, filled with disbelief at what they had just witnessed. Of all the flummoxing encounters they had experienced so far, this would be the tale Father would not believe. Ybbub slowly raised his noggin up from cover, peeking to make sure the battle had indeed ceased.

"Alright, Tootie. A whale of a time we've had now. A whale of a time. I know ya didn't mean those nasty names ya called me." He turned about to the four girls and whispered, "That pie really wasn't that good, to be honest. Too many blueberries." A battle cry rang out as the old woman ran out of the cottage, holding a broom high above her gray head as if it were a battle axe.

"I heard that, you old milk curd, island snoozer, shamrock eatin,' pie thieving . . ." She violently continued with no restraint to beat the giant with strike after strike using the old wooden broom. With each hit, the giant exploded with dust as if she were cleaning the household rugs during springtime. Ybbub then knelt to a knee and did his best to protect himself.

"Tootie! I said I'm sorry!" Smack! Thump! Bang! Boom!

An 8 foot giant was being thrashed by an old maid with a wooden broom. A sad sight this was indeed, all four girls thought. This is who they had begged and pleaded with to lead them heroically through the Black Ghost Forest. The old lady shouted as she continued to swing with all her might, "Do ya got any idea how long it took me to make that pie? It was for . . ."

An older man then appeared from the back of the cottage carrying two wooden pails in his hands. "Aye yi yi! Tootie, what's a all a des pots a doin here a lyinnnn abooooout?" No more than sixty-five, the man stood there with a white bushy moustache, gray stringy hair past his ears, and a brown leather arming cap on his head. He wore an old white shirt that was tucked into his tight dark green britches. "Aye, Ybbub! Good to a see you my old a friend! Aye, Tootie my a dear. Why are a you a beating 'im wif da broom?" He spoke with a unique and distinct accent that's believed to be in the old Magyar tongue. Just to hear him speak was a thrill all its own. It certainly made one truly focus every time his lips moved so that if you did not, the whole conversation would be lost.

The old lady's hair was now even more messy, matching her disheveled apron. She replied with a look of vengeance toward her husband, "Not another word from you, Mr. Wheat. Unless you'd like to be dusted as well!" She then turned and noticed all four girls who stood there with mouths dropped, watching in amazement. Unbeknownst to the old lady, they had been viewing the pathetic scolding and reprimand the entire time. The old woman frantically fixed her apron properly, smoothed back her hair in its rightful place, and walked toward them. Acting now as if nothing had happened, she had become a completely different person. She curtsied and began to speak gently. "And who might these sweet, well-mannered little angels be?"

Ybbub, still picking the straw out of his beard, carefully said, "That's what I was try'n to tell ya, but ya kept beat'n me with the broom." Cough! Cough!

The old man walked over to Ybbub and began dusting him off. "I saved 'em from them Beo Creatlaches," Ybbub explained. "Them bloody things 'bout got the best of 'em 'til ol' Ybbub showed up."

Tootie marched over and smacked Ybbub on the shoulder as a mother would her child. "Ybbub, do not use that type of language in front of the lit'l lasses. You'll corrupt their youthful, innocent ears."

Ybbub began rubbing his shoulder as he stood up and walked over to the girls. "They're lookin' for their ma and da. They haven't gotten the slightest clue what happened to 'em or where they may be. Both just . . . disappeared."

Both the old man and woman shook their heads in disbelief as the sight of the four girls began to break their hearts. Sophia stepped forward and said, "Ybbub's right. We don't know where they are. They were taken about a day ago during the night. We followed a trail into the Black Ghost Forest, and that's where we met him." Ybbub smiled as Sophia pointed toward the bruised giant.

Sarah Honey cautiously walked up to Tootie and gently tugged on the bottom of her apron. "Your very pretty."

Placing her hand on her chest in awe, Tootie lovingly replied, "Oh my dear, sweet child. Thank you. What wonderful little ladies we have here. Please, children, come inside and get warm." Tootie escorted the girls inside the cottage and called for her husband. "Mr. Wheat! Mr. Wheat!" The old man noticed the sword Sophia had tucked in her belt. Unable to conceal it due to losing her mother's quilt in the river, it now shined and glistened in the evening sun. "Augustus!" Tootie called again to her husband. The old man had been so mesmerized studying the hilt that he was unaware his loving wife had been calling him. "Aye, yes me dear. I'm a coming!" Tootie then advised him to fetch two wooden pails of milk and bring them inside for the girls. "Aye, yes me dear. As you a wish!"

Tootie then gave him another order. "And pick up all these pots and pans!" The four girls were now inside with Mrs. Wheat who had shut the door behind them.

Mr. Wheat and Ybbub walked to the stable and fetched the milk. As they walked back, Mr. Wheat curiously asked as they picked up the pots and pans, "Ybbub. That a sword. Where did a she get a that?"

Continuing to walk beside him, Ybbub said, "Well um, she never really said, Augustus. I asked her, but that lit'l angel never gave word about it."

With a suspicious manner, Mr. Wheat looked over at Ybbub and whispered, "Dat a sword, Ybbub. Dat golden hilt. Dat a red jewel. Aye recognize dat a sword."

Ybbub interrupted him with an admiring laugh and interjected, "Oh yes, Augustus, now that is a fine dragon pok'a if I ever did see one. It's a nasty shame too—the point of the blade is chipped. That lit'l lass would've gutted me like a bloody pig! Jabbed it right into me belly she did."

Mr. Wheat paused in his tracks as he instantly dropped the two wooden pails filled with milk to the ground. With a grin, he turned to Ybbub. "Dat blade, Ybbub. Dat lit'l young'n . . ."

Ybbub, who had become confused, began to rub his long, stringy beard. "What are ya jabber'n about?"

Mr. Wheat picked up the pails once more. "Dat sword, Ybbub. Dat sword belongs to a brave, courageous, and fearless knight—a knight dat led an army a to battle an entire nation. He led da entire a Royal Golden Eagle Army."

Ybbub's eyes opened wide as he turned his head and dropped his jaw. "Who was this knight, Augustus?" Now at the entrance of the door to the cottage, Mr. Wheat whispered profoundly, "Ybbub, my old a friend, the master of that a sword was a Protector of da Pure and Avenger to da Wicked. Sir Daniel . . . da Fearless."

Chapter Eleven

A Name That Summons Evil

A lovely fire engulfed the oak logs embedded in the fireplace as it crackled with glows of red, yellow, and orange. As the sun began to descend, Mrs. Wheat placed the girls' tattered stockings and wet quilts along the mantel to dry them out from their long, excruciating journey. Along with the smoke of the burning firewood, the cottage was consumed with the pleasant aroma of what many would like to fancy a well-established bakery.

"Would you like another one, my deary?" asked Tootie.

"Yes, Mrs. Wheat," Savannah responded.

"Oh, you sweet angel. What lovely manners these young ladies have." Tootie then placed another slice of blueberry pie on Savannah's plate. "You just call me Aunt Tootie."

All four girls happily filled their vacant, rumbling bellies with delicious blueberry pie, buttery peach cobbler, and a helping of cinnamon dough sticks dipped in sugary glaze. Each of them ate as if it were their last meal indeed.

Scarlett appeared to have taken pleasure in the private bakery more than the others—noticeably due to half the desserts covering her face while still chewing her food at the table.

"Stop chewing like that, Scarlett. You're making me sick," Savannah said with a curled lip of disapproval. Smears of chocolate, blueberry filling, and icing covered her entire face. Although nothing had been served with frosting yet, somehow it was caked on her left cheek. One thing was for sure. If there were sweets, Scarlett would find them. She resembled a cake, indeed, where the only decor she lacked were the candles. More than likely, Scarlett would have eaten them as well due to the heavenly cooking that Mrs. Wheat could conjure.

Mr. Wheat shuffled through the door carrying the two wooden pails of freshly gathered milk. "Here you go, my a dear. Some a fresh milk for our a guests."

Mrs. Wheat filled four cups to the brim with the coldest, sweetest cow pull the girls had ever tasted. Poor Sarah Honey, who barely had the strength to lift her glass, left it on the table and began drinking it as a house cat would from a saucer. After she finally was able to take a sip, she lifted her head to show a thick, white moustache painted along her top lip. Mr. Wheat with a jolly laugh said, "Now dats how you a do it, my a lit'l Honey! Hahahaha!"

Cleverly, Ybbub cautiously slipped through the doorway, peeking his head through its crack as if checking for safe passage. Mimicking a mouse (although he feared them dearly), he slithered into the living quarters, barely noticed. The 8 foot giant was trying his best to avoid another broomstick beating and tongue lashing if that was at all possible. There was a large, ladle-size lump atop his head, caused by the outrageous beating inflicted by the floury hands of Mrs. Wheat. Who knows what might have taken place if the four girls had not been standing there. Ybbub tiptoed unnoticed past the wooden chairs, across the sheepskin rug, and over to the fireplace. Tootie remained in the kitchen, continuing to roll dough near the stove, creating another treat for her well-mannered company.

Ybbub slowly sat down by the fireplace in the corner, believing in his mind that he was still undetected. *Well done!* he thought to himself as he warmed his huge bearskin-covered feet by the beaming fire.

"You're a lot brave 'a than I thought ya were," Tootie calmly told Ybbub with her back still turned to him.

He began stuttering while giving a quick response. "Um . . . Aye . . . Uh."

Tootie turned and threw a wet rag at him. "Hush! Do ya realize how silly ya sound? Stop that Gaelic gibberish!"

Ybbub felt somewhat relieved that even though he had been inside for only thirty seconds, that time had been far longer than what he imagined he would be given inside. "Aye." Sniff. Sniff. "Is that blueberry pie I smell? Oh, now that's lovely it 'tis," Ybbub mumbled while sniffing aggressively in the air like a hunting dog on the trail of its game. Mrs. Wheat swiftly turned around toward him and gave a look that would have struck fear in all the Knights of the Round Table.

While sitting at the table finishing her fifth cinnamon dough stick, Scarlett casually asked, "What was that word you said earlier, Sophia? Oldplumb?" Sophia raised her head from her plate, bearing a look as if a secret had been announced.

Savannah spoke up. "No, Scarlett. It was Olcnom. Not Oldplumb." The room became silently numb and no one made a sound.

Mr. Wheat, who was sitting in his chair in front of the fireplace while smoking his wooden pipe, leaped up and rushed to the table. "Sssssshhhhhhh! No! No! Do not a say dat a word!" He then frantically hurried to the window and closed the thick, wooden shutters.

All eyes became fixated on Mr. Wheat as he slowly walked toward the girls who were sitting at the table. Completely ignorant and unaware of what they had just done, they could see the sweat running from Augustus's brow down to his nose. He turned to the windows for a quick glance and then back to the girls. Wiping his nose, he knelt down to whisper among them, "Please don't a say dat a name again." He held his finger to his lips while his ungroomed, gray and white moustache protruded on each side. No more did the sunshine creep through the shutters along the windows due to the thickness of the night. Mr. Wheat proceeded to show his nervousness while trying not to frighten his young guests. He tensely rubbed his chin, turned, and gave Mrs. Wheat a look of occupied regret. The riddled topic the old man grudgingly decided to speak about held no vacancy within himself. With that said, since the name had been spoken, it must reluctantly be addressed.

Mr. Wheat motioned for the girls to gather in close, all while still sitting among each other at the crumb-covered kitchen table. Ybbub chose to remain seated next to the fire, refusing to engage in such a dreadful and horrifying discussion. He chose rather to listen from afar off.

"Where did a you hear dat a name?" Mr. Wheat said, whispering as quietly as possible with a deep, raspy voice. Usually when he spoke, it was high-pitched, joyful, and in the most unusual accent. Sophia knew at this moment that the name she heard had a deeper meaning than what she had thought before. The old man was not joyful but fearful.

"I heard . . ." Sophia began. Augustus raised his hands and began to plead for Sophia to lower her voice.

"Dat. Dat. Dat. Sssshhhhhh! Quiet, please," he whispered as he began to nervously scan the room.

"Sophia heard Father's voice whisper it in her ear after they disappeared or something," Scarlett said with a mouthful of the rest of Savannah's peach cobbler. Mrs. Wheat placed her hand over her mouth in shock.

"I did," Sophia said hesitantly. "I know it sounds silly. While standing in the doorway after they vanished,

I . . . I . . . I heard his voice whisper it in my ear." Sophia looked down at her plate, took her fork, and began to play with the crumps that lay wasted. Within her, she was awaiting crude mockery from those in the room due to the silliness of the mentioning of her claim. No laughter was heard from the old man.

"You heard . . . your father a whisper dat?" Mr. Wheat asked.

Sophia slowly raised her head and nodded yes as she gently sat the fork back down on her plate.

Savannah spoke up while wiping Sarah Honey's face. "Mr. Wheat, what is it that she heard Father whisper in her ear?"

Mr. Wheat sat in the wooden chair next to Sophia at the table while putting his hands together in a praying manner. "Children, aye want you to a listen to a me carefully. Dis a place is a pure evil, nothing but vileness, viciousness, and destruction dwell at a dis awful place."

Ybbub looked from the fireplace as he rubbed the back of his neck, making his unpleasant feelings inside viewable.

"Augustus, I don't think the lit'l ladies . . ." Tootie interjected while wiping the chocolate icing from Scarlett's face with her apron.

"No, Tootie! No! Dey a come dis a far. Dey need a to know da truth," Mr. Wheat said, slamming his balled fist violently on the table. It was because he was interrupted but because he was angry that their sweet pure minds would now be hindered about such a dismal place. The place was not imaginary, make-believe, or a simple grim story. It 'twas a nightmare that never seemed to slumber or rest.

Tootie grew weary that the younger girls, especially Sarah Honey, would become terrified hearing of such a place. She sat down with Savannah and Sarah as she held them close, clinging to them as if they were her own.

"Do you think that's where they are?" Sophia whispered. Augustus turned and looked at Ybbub as they both contemplated the terrible possible reality of their poor mother and father. An eerie silence filled the cold, stony cottage as Mr. Wheat finally gathered the courage to continue.

"To even a speak it brings a destruction and doom," he said. "Dis a place is a nowhere for you lit'l angels to a go. Not a even five thousand of a da most daring and courageous knights would venture a out to dis kingdom." Mr. Wheat's hands began to shake. "Its Lord is a unknown to a be duine or devil. Beo or dead. Creature or spirit. All da fearful eyes dat have a laid upon a his black soul cannot a deny any of da possibilities. Any possibility except a for a one—mercy. Never has he bestowed a mercy on anyone or a anything."

Sitting in his wooden chair, Augustus appeared to hold back tears as his bloodshot eyes began to fill with what one would describe as pain and anguish. "Many a brave men have perished and a sacrificed themselves trying to a conquer dis a fiend. Dis ruler of that kingdom you spoke of."

Sarah Honey got up and placed her hand on Mr. Wheat's back, seeing that he was growing increasingly distressed. As the old man tried to harness what he thought were embarrassing emotions, Sophia asked the glaring question all four girls wondered in their hearts. "Who is it? Who is this awful man . . . creature . . . thing?"

Mr. Wheat, able to defeat the viewable depression within himself, answered her daunting request. "Dey call a him exactly what he is—Sin! Ri Sin! Lord Sin of da kingdom founded upon war and strife."

A terrible piercing screech suddenly echoed just outside the stone cottage. Each screech was followed by another simultaneously in what sounded like four or five had now surrounded them. Mr. Wheat then shoved back the chair and rushed to the shuttered window to catch a peek of whoever or whatever was causing such a gut-churning uproar. Through the moonlight he could see fowl creatures circling the cottage where there was a thunderous bang at the front door that knocked dust clear across the room.

"Quick, Ybbub, brace da door!" Augustus shouted. Ybbub dashed across the room and held the large, now-splintered door with all his giant might. "Aye yi yi! Da window! Look!"

Sarah Honey screamed, motioning frantically to the window as the shutters began to burst open. They all saw a terrible sight as several bony arms of the Beo Creatlache began reaching inside, grabbing whatever and whoever they could clutch. Tootie swiftly took Sarah and Savannah by the hand and darted toward the fireplace. As they passed by the window, Sarah tripped over a spindle that had tipped over onto the floor. Trying to get to her feet, a Creatlache caught a handful of her dress and began to yank her through the window. “Help, Tootie! Help me!” poor Sarah Honey cried in fright. Tootie quickly grabbed her hand and pulled with all her might to keep her from the dead’s deadly hold. The fabric of her dress ripped, and they both fell backward on top of the spindle.

“Ouch!” Tootie shouted as she landed on top of something that was lying in the floor. It ‘twas an iron skillet that Ybbub had retrieved from the front yard earlier. Without hesitation, the old lady placed her favorite weapon of choice into her flour-covered hand. She took the skillet and threw it like a tomahawk directly at the Beo Creatlache in the window. Ding! It knocked its head clear off its shoulders. Mrs. Wheat helped Sarah Honey up, and where she and the girls ran toward the fireplace and hid behind a large wooden chest.

They heard the chilling sound of chopping and slashing as the evil intruders violently strained to gain access inside. It did not take long before they accomplished their devout goal. Suddenly several of the skeletons climbed through.

“Aye yi yi! Dey got in!” Augustus yelled as he dashed to the wooden chest where Tootie and the girls were hiding. With no time to waste, he forcefully tried to raise the top. “Aye yi yi! It’s a locked! Tootie, where is da key?”

Mrs. Wheat screamed, “Ya put it under the chest so you would remember where it ‘twas if ya needed it!”

The old man quickly retrieved the key and desperately unlocked the chest. He reached inside and pulled out a wooden stick wrapped in leather that had a long iron-linked chain attached. As he lifted the intimidating item from the chest, a spiked iron metal ball swayed at the end of the chain. Sophia watched. She was familiar with the weapon due to seeing flags and paintings in the village kingdom. After asking Father what it was, he advised her that the fearful weapon was called a mace.

It appeared that the entity of evil had now encompassed the entire cottage, not leaving an inch to spare. Windows continued to be struck as well as the door that Ybbub was still holding. Evil creatures continued to pry and pull from the outside.

"You cursed, bloody demons! Ya rotten worm canker'n buggers!" Ybbub shouted while bracing with all his strength. The fire then blew out as a heavy gust of wind shot through the tightly sealed, mudded cottage. Three Creatlaches covered in black soot fell through the chimney. They were all dressed in disheveled armor and equipped with rusty blades.

Sophia finally drew her father's sword from her belt and held it up with both hands, trembling with fear. The creatures rushed toward her with blades pointing like an army charging into battle. She grew motionless as her body locked, and fright reigned supreme. Mr. Wheat saw the look on her little face and was aware she could not comprehend the effects of warfare. He leaped over to her as the Creatlaches began to subdue Sophia, the eldest of the four girls. With mace in hand, Mr. Wheat swung the iron wrecking ball, causing a mighty fatal blow to the charging demons.

Bones flew all over the room as he yelled, "Get back, Sophia! Dat was a too close!"

More Creatlaches came in through the window as the wooden latch had dwindled to nothing but splinters. They were all wielding weapons with malice and intent to cause pain or worse—possessing the desire to kill, to kill at all costs. Two of the possessed skeletons dashed through as Ybbub saw them pass by. Ybbub quickly grabbed the kitchen table with one hand and braced it against the damaged front door. The giant was swift as a banshee, grabbing both Creatlaches by the neck just before they made it to Scarlett who was standing near the cupboard. With each hand full of visible vertebra, Ybbub viscously slammed the two Creatlaches together. Piles of bones lay motionless on his bearskin-covered feet.

Mixtures of screams and smoke filled the cottage air while lifeless bones decorated the Wheats' floor. While gazing about the room, Sophia beheld a shadow growing and swallowing her own that was painted along the dusty wooden floor. Prancing from behind was a much taller skeleton that had made its way inside. Holding two swords in its bony hands, the lanky imp ran toward her. Augustus and Ybbub were occupied on the other side of the cottage as they fought diligently while trying to keep more from gaining entry.

Just as the Creatlache raised its rusty swords, Sophia closed her eyes and held her father's blade into the air—a remarkable reflex that resulted in a positive defense. Unfortunately, the force dislodged the sword from her hands. As the creature crept toward her, Scarlett Belle knew she could not watch from the kitchen any longer. She looked to her left and saw a half-filled flour sack that Mrs. Wheat had been using to make her delicious treats. Sophia stood before the approaching foe as it raised its two swords once again. She was unable to retrieve her weapon as it lay on the ground. Scarlett scurried to the flour sack and lifted it from the counter. Swinging desperately with all her might, the flour hit directly into the skeleton's ribs, causing it to tumble to the ground. A white cloud now consumed the battlefield throughout the quarters.

On the other side of the room, Sarah Honey shouted, "Ybbub, behind you!" Like a flash of lightning, the giant turned, laying hold of the Creatlache's fleshless skull. Letting out a boisterous roar like that of a Urus Arctos bear, Ybbub crushed the skull as if it were a ripe melon. The mythical giant had finally fulfilled at least one of the tall tales the girls grew up hearing from Father. It was a terrible but fascinating sight to witness such an act of strength.

The reckless commotion inside the stony walls had ceased. Not a single sound was heard from outside nor in. The clinging of the armor, racket of the bones, and screams of the fearful had ceased to a humming pitch known as the sound of silence. Each attempted to catch their breaths as their hearts raced from the terrorizing fight—a fight that none had prepared for but endured, nonetheless. A sudden thud on the roof was heard as screeching echoed in the distance. The cottage had become dark and dim with only the eerie moonlight shining in through the splintered shutters.

Mr. Wheat whispered as he carefully scanned the room, "Everyone okay?" All responded with a declaration of a not-so-assuring "Aye." Savannah pulled herself up from behind the old wooden chest and ran to Mr. Wheat. "Oh my! Your arm!" Unmindful and mentally dazed due to the vast effects of combat, Mr. Wheat had received a rather nasty gash just below his shoulder along his left arm. Blood continued to profusely gush, painting shades of red on the deadly mace he firmly grasped in his now scarlet-stained hand.

As he looked down and viewed the menacing sight, Mr. Wheat babbled, "Aye yi yi." Slowly he slumped to the bloodied floor. While lying there gazing up at the ceiling with the moonlight shining upon him, he whispered, "Don't a no one a say dat a name again . . . Rendben."

Ybbub nodded his large noggin and gave the girls a wink as he patted Savannah on the head. "Agreed, fella. Agreed."

Chapter Twelve

One's Past Revealed to Lead the Present

Sophia and Mrs. Wheat held the torn kitchen rags firmly against Augustus's arm as they attempted to clot the wound before he lost any more blood. "Hurry, fetch another one, deary!" yelled Tootie as Savannah watched in disbelief. Blood soaked through the rags as it ran over both their hands.

Ybbub began picking up the dry bones from their skirmish as if collecting firewood, tucking them beneath his arms. He peeked out the window and gave a report: "Not a soul outside. Just the dreadful fog and trees, my lit'l lasses."

The adrenaline in each of them began to fade like sap slowly flowing down the flaky bark to the roots of a pine tree. The youthful girls had never experienced such fatigue like the sluggish effects of warfare and the traumatic stress it undoubtedly harbors.

Sophia tried her best to hold pressure on Augustus's arm, not wishing to cause any further damage. The old man looked at her for a moment and determined that the truth could no longer be kept a secret. Mr. Wheat abruptly said, "Ya look a just lik'a yur father." She suddenly released pressure and dropped the rag. Lifting her head, she looked the wounded elder in the eyes and took several steps back. Ybbub immediately dropped the wagon-sized load of bones to the floor. "My . . . my father?" Sophia said with an expression brought to life by the light that pierced her through the shattered window. The glow danced upon the golden hilt of her father's sword as if sent down from grace above. "Aye. Yur a father. You a look just a like 'im," he replied while trying to hold back the constant sting of his newly acquired wound.

"You knew my father?" Sophia said, looking at Savannah who stood by Mrs. Wheat with the other two sisters. "Aye. Dat aye did. Sir Daniel. Sir Daniel da Fearless," he painfully whispered while clinching his arm for relief. Scarlett stepped toward him. "Did you say Sir Daniel the Fearless? Our father was a stablehand, a farmer, a tiller of the ground—not a knight."

Savannah looked at Scarlett and held her finger up to her lips. "Shush."

Eyeing Sophia, Scarlett said, "Sophia would often go with Father to the village, but sometimes he would simply tell her that she couldn't go. We would ask Mother why he had to leave, but she would often be short and say he was simply who the village needed."

All four girls stood there confused, pondering in their hearts if what they had just heard was indeed the gospel truth. "I have never heard Father called that before," said Sarah Honey. Scarlett grew aggravated and could no longer contain the steam that pressurized inside her. "Because it's not true, Sarah!" Savannah politely declined the title bestowed upon her father. "Mr. Wheat, I regret to inform you that I believe you are mistaken. I'm dearly sorry."

"Dat sword." Augustus exclaimed while pointing toward Sophia. Full attention was set upon the oldest of the four. Feeling the beaming stare of each accompanying soul in her midst, Sophia glanced down at the golden hilt. The sword seemed to shine and shimmer like never before. The old man began to pull himself up off the cold, blood-stained floor as Ybbub walked over to carefully assist him to his feet.

"Dat a sword you possess. Is dat a yur a father's?"

Scanning the room, trying to think of a logical explanation, Sophia simply whispered, "Why?"

With a smile stretched across his face that could not be hidden behind the bushy, gray moustache, Mr. Wheat said, "Lit'l angel, dat a sword's master was a Protector of da Pure and Avenger to da Wicked."

Tootie placed her hand on Mr. Wheat's back and chest, trying to silence him from further inflicting stress upon their guests. "Now Augustus, let's not frigh . . ."

Once more he slammed his fist. "Tootie! Dey need to a know who der father is!" Mr. Wheat winced in pain and attempted to calm himself as he began to unveil the shocking reality regarding their father.

Ybbub walked over to the mantel and began stacking wood to burn in the fireplace. The light from the bright flame flickered, casting a large silhouette of the four girls, Tootie, and Mr. Wheat against the stony wall. The wounded old man firmly held the reins of their immediate attention. They were about to hear who their father really was.

"Aye a knew yur a father. Aye a have known Sir Daniel for a long, long time." With his back turned toward them, he shuffled over to the wooden chest near the fireplace. It was the same wooden chest where he had obtained his deadly mace earlier. He motioned for Ybbub to open it as the chest made a rackety sound. Mr. Wheat reached down and began to move things about inside. Finally, he retrieved a coveted item, swaddled in cloth as if it had been tucked away in its resting place for ages. Grimacing as he turned around from the pain and exhaustion, he uncannily wore a slight grin on his tattered, wrinkled face. Ybbub towered above Mr. Wheat as he crouched over with an interesting smile while a glaring twinkle shined in his eye that glimmered clear across the room.

The old man unfolded the tightly wrapped treasure as thick dust wafted into the already smoky air. As the stars glistened throughout the dark, cloudless night, so too did this beloved trophy he embraced. The reflection of the smoldering fire cast upon the item as he whispered, "Aye a served with a yur a father. Many years ago."

In his dry, blood-stained hands, Mr. Wheat cradled a great helm helmet forged long ago from iron and overlayed with a pure sheet of solid gold. At the face of the helmet was etched a golden eagle with its head and beak facing downward, overlapping the wearer's nose. Its wings spread to each outer side of the eyes as its tail protruded above the crown. Each feather was crafted with precision and detail. Within the golden eagle's eyes were two red gems resembling those fashioned on Sophia's father's sword.

Augustus walked over to the girls and gently placed the battle-worn helmet on the window frame. There was a pause as the old man contemplated in his soul the sudden decision to reveal the past from long ago. "Aye was a captain in da Royal Golden Eagle Army. Me and a yur father, Sir Daniel, served together. We fought to defend dis a land. Fought to a defend it from da wickedness dat a now chokes it. Defend it from da same evil dat has taken yur dear mother and a father!"

Savannah spoke up. "Did you know my mother as well?"

Mr. Wheat turned and walked toward her while gently touching her fair cheek with his hand as he smiled. "Aye. Dat aye did. You my a lit'l angel hold her sweet, beautiful reflection as if she were standing right a before me." Savannah's smile grew much larger as she began to wipe a tear from her eye.

As Sophia glanced at the helmet and then back to her

father's sword she interjected, "Where could they be? You must know. Why have they both disappeared?"

Augustus slowly walked back over to the helmet and turned in Sophia's direction. "My lit'l angel, dey have a not a disappeared. Dey have a been taken!"

Scarlett leaped from Tootie's warm, comforting embrace and shouted, "To Olc . . ."

Mr. Wheat frantically raised his arm to prevent yet another ignorant and costly mistake. "Ssshhh. Dat dat dat, Aye am afraid so, lit'l angels. Ayes afraid so."

Ybbub, staring deeply into the warm, blazing fire no longer stayed silent. "That place. 'Tis engulfed with unimaginable misery, things that are too—too troubling for even the most reckless warrior. Believe you me, it's no place to desire."

Sophia looked at her three sisters as they all grew weary of the thought that all hope was lost. She was weary of the sick feeling that never again would they be tucked into bed by Father and told another tall tale. Never again would they feel the warm, loving embrace of Mother's hug. The depressing and constant imagery of them being held captive or worse felt like a serpent wrapping itself around their consciousness, choking what hope remained to a lifeless falsehood. The room felt just like that—lifeless and miserable, consumed by the likelihood they would never see their parents again.

Sophia quickly turned to Augustus as her braid whipped across her back. "Help us," Mr. Wheat." She clutched his arm and stared at the bloody floor as Ybbub walked over where they were all standing, away from the fireplace. "Mr.

Wheat, if you say my father was as fearless as you claim, then you undoubtedly know he would charge unaccompanied into that devilish place with this sword in his hand and contest whoever stood before him. He would dare to fight to save us. He would dare to fight to save you!"

Shaken, Mr. Wheat had been presented with wisdom and truth from a young girl not yet twenty. Rubbing his unshaven face, he mumbled, "My lit'l angels, aye a am an old man. A shell of what aye a used to be. Ya sweet darlin' girls. Dat is a no a place fur a you to venture. Only death and a destruction are what a you will a find." He then began to shake his head, "No. No. No. Aye can't."

The room was spent with tension as it seemed courage was harbored only within the four little girls. Just as her mother's gift at the bottom of the river grave, there was nothing Sophia felt could be done as it sank to the deep. Ybbub began rubbing his face with his calloused hands, feeling the guilt that flowed through his thick veins—guilt that he had led them all this way for no gain.

"I know that he and mother would face all the evil, destruction, pestilences, and wickedness for each one of us." Sophia pulled the sword from her belt and firmly held it before her face. Beholding her father's sword, she once again noticed each dent, scratch, mark, stain, and chip. Hearing the identity of her beloved father, she felt even more empowered by the blade. "My mother and father would not run from Sin. They would confront him."

Mr. Wheat anxiously turned his back to them all as they

awaited his final response. His helmet sat in front of him as he became lost in the memories of his forgotten past. Sophia stepped toward him. "Whether you go with us or not, I'm going there." As Sophia stood there with sword in hand, Savannah, Scarlett, and Sarah Honey lined up behind her as if ready to sound the charge into battle. They were no longer afraid or conflicted about whether to continue their crusade. They knew within that they must stay together. All of them stood there awaiting Mr. Wheat's final say.

Tootie stood next to her husband as she feared the outcome of such an unfavorable journey. She placed her hand on top of his as they both rested on the cool, dented helmet the girls' father once proudly and bravely wore. Turning to him as tears ran down her flour-covered cheeks, Tootie nodded and said, "Augustus, those lit'l dearies need you. Daniel and Noel need you. You don't have a choice, Augustus."

Moving his hand from the helmet, Augustus turned back toward the girls and Ybbub, leaving a blood-stained handprint on top of the crown. The old man beheld four young girls, nicely fitted in hand-sewn dresses and braided hair. His beating heart felt pierced, bludgeoned by their sweet innocence and willfulness to tread into the realm of evil on behalf of their loved ones. He could not dare allow them to go alone. Glancing at them all, he said, "Aye yi yi. Aye. Aye will a help you."

Chapter Thirteen

An Honorable Service Indeed

It was not a full night's rest, but what little sleep they harvested was needed. The sun began to rise as the morning fog and winter chill nipped at each of the girls' noses. "Okay, my lit'l dearies. Ya should have enough to a do ya. Wrap them up tight," said Mr. Wheat.

Tootie assisted the girls, filling each of their knitted bags. Walking over to Scarlett, she saw her hunched over, indulging in her food just prepared for their departure. "Don't eat it all now, my deary," she said, tapping her on the head.

There were cakes, cookies, breads, and the most scrumptious of all—Tootie's specialty, monkey pudding. It was a delicious recipe of cow pull (milk), a peanut spread, sugar, flour, and blueberries—chilled after placing it in the snow and preparing it in a small, wooden cup the size of your hand. Tootie exhibited more than pride regarding her skills as a cook and baker. There was, in fact, an obvious reason for Mr. Wheat's round, protruding belly.

Ybbub, just a few nails from finishing securing the window that had been broken, kept eyeing Tootie's creations in the kitchen while she baked. Tootie observed him in the corner of her eye as she suddenly stuck her gray head out the window. Ybbub reluctantly waved as he looked back, continuing to act as if he was hard at work putting on the concluding touches.

"Oh, alright," Tootie said. "Come here, you!" Tootie then stuffed an empty flour sack full of the same spoils she had prepared for the girls and handed it to him through the window.

"Oh my! Ar scath a cheile a mhaireann na daoine," Ybbub said in a kind soft voice after retrieving the filled sack.

"What in the heavens does that mean?" Tootie asked with a jumbled look about her face.

"Tootie, my deary, that's the old language of our forefathers. It means under the shadow of each other, people survive."

Tootie sarcastically put her hands together with fingers laced to her cheek and said in a mocking voice, "Oh isn't that lovely."

Ybbub's smile turned to a frown as he began to walk away, feeling displeased with her unaffectionate reaction. The old woman stuck her head back out the window and yelled for Ybbub. He turned and walked back to the window, hoping for a word of appreciation regarding his poetic compliment. As he leaned down to her, Tootie said, "Here's ya more treat!" There was the sound of a thump, followed by a white cloud that engulfed Ybbub's entire head, round nose, and what used to be brown beard. "Haha! Now there's one for the road!" she said while cackling uncontrollably.

"Why did ya have ta do that, Tootie? What a waste of scrumptious flour," he mumbled while wiping the flour from his face and clothes.

Scarlett and Sarah Honey tried to hold back their laughter but failed to do so, while Savannah appeared not so amused. She ran outside and bid to aid the lovable titan with cleaning up. "Here, let me help you." she said while dusting the flour off his bear fur shirt. After helping him the best she could, Savannah went back into the cottage to stitch Sarah's dress that had been torn throughout the night's skirmish.

Tootie watched her with amazement. She marveled at how well-skilled she was with a needle and thread. "Why you're quite the mender, my lit'l deary. Betta than I am you are."

Before their lives changed upon the disappearance of their mother and father, Savannah Gene was regarded as the household seamstress. Noel, her mother, had educated her in the art of stitching, and to say she was good at it would be an implication of sarcasm. Every special occasion she would provide genuine gifts created by her steady, gentle hand.

After mending Sarah's dress, Savannah walked over to Mrs. Wheat in the kitchen and kindly offered her a gift.

Giving her a small, yellow butterfly, she said, "I wanted to give you this. I know it isn't much, but it's the least I can do to repay all your generosity."

Tootie's eyes became filled with tears as she pulled Savannah in and gave her a hug. "Oh, it's lovely, my lit'l deary. Bless your lit'l heart. Bless you." While holding her, Tootie appeared troubled within herself as the tears flowed down her face. The gesture appeared to have released emotions that were hidden deep within the old woman's soul. "Oh, how much you remind me of . . ."

Ybbub stuck his head back through the window. "Tootie! Augustus is ready for the rest of the supplies." Mrs. Wheat quickly wiped the tears away and pulled herself back to reality. Although she felt thankful for the small sewn gift, the biggest blessing she had received was the new relationship that filled a void deep within her heart that she thought would be empty for the rest of her life.

Sophia sat still in the wooden chair by the fireplace, unaware of what was taking place around her. The jokes, the laughter, the hugs—none of it resonated inside her mind. She was now lost in the hypnotizing flames as her thoughts still wandered just as they had in the forest. Silent she sat, pondering and contemplating as the charred logs burned—contemplating if she truly possessed the ability to overcome whatever lay ahead of her. To do exactly what she said she would do several hours earlier. To confront whatever and whoever stood between her and her loved ones.

Ybbub and Mr. Wheat were now out back in the stable

loading their packs on Augustus's stubborn donkey, Gus. He was a hateful beast that looked to be as old as Mr. Wheat himself. Both shared many similarities in the confines of being old, stubborn, and worst of all, smelly. At the end of a list of negative traits, both possessed another similar virtue portrayed through the years. Reliable. Being stubborn is not a bad virtue if it firmly roots the possessor from unwavering their morals and principles.

Several leather bags, cloth sacks, as well as cookware consisting of pots and pans were draped across old Gus's back. Heehaw! Heehaw! Mr. Wheat slapped Gus's rear end as if he were a child misbehaving, and shouted, "Ah shut up, ya stubborn donkey!" Ybbub patted the top of Gus's head as he comforted him. "Leave that lit'l fella alone. He's a good lad he is." Mr. Wheat rolled his eyes as he continued to cinch the leather straps to secure their supplies.

The crisp full morning had finally set in the Black Ghost Forest. Sophia finally walked outside the cottage, and a sudden thought entered her wondering mind. If the haunted, forbidden forest was such a terrible place, why did such loving and charitable people choose to make it their home? There was no time for such questions as they all prepared themselves for the excursion. The crows began to caw among the treetops as they were the only life outside the Wheats' humble abode. They inflicted an eerie stare with their black, beady eyes as if scouting the supplies, weaponry, and potency.

"Okey doke. Aye a believe dat will a do it." Augustus began to routinely check the provisions with his hands placed on the sides of his round, protruding belly. "Let a me see here. Kettles, pans, flour, flint, canvas, quilts, candles, rope, and . . . a monkey pudding." Ybbub chuckled, watching him with a grin. Mr. Wheat had already checked the supplies three times before this fourth inspection. Instead of making things worse, Ybbub let the old man be about his business. Not daring to distract, the giant approached Mr. Wheat as he bent down with his back facing the girls while they finished packing. "Augustus, do ya really think we can find this place? Are . . . are we doin' them lit'l angels a favor escortin 'em there?" Mr. Wheat paused for a moment as he looked down. "And if we do make it there, then what?" Ybbub whispered.

Augustus lifted his head and fixed his eyes on three of the girls as they stood near the well. Each had long brown hair, colorful but now stained dresses, and smiles as they watched the hogs rolling in the pen. A feeling of responsibility and eagerness overflowed his old beating heart with the desire to help the poor, innocent darlins. "Ybbub, Dem youngins ain't a got a nobody now. We are a all dey a got. Did a you see der a faces? Ybbub, aye a know how it a feels to a lose a someone. We are all dey a got."

Ybbub gently placed his hand on his dear friend's shoulder and gave a reassuring wink. "Grand it 'tis, Augustus. An honorable service we now have indeed."

Chapter Fourteen

The Bitter Taste of Departure

The cool wind blew strong, trying its best to pierce through their quilts and capes wrapped around them. Morning frost gave the miserable forest an apparent shine as the grass appeared crystalized. Tootie met the girls outside, instructing them on the do's and do nots as if she were their granny of old. "Remember now, don't eat ya food in one setting, dearies—especially you, Scarlett." Scarlett rolled her eyes with a sneaky grin as if pleading guilty. "I won't." Realism had now sprouted in each of their little minds that they were about to march toward the most undesired place known to man.

What these unfortunate poor girls had known their entire lives had been altered within a couple of days—a life filled with laughing, playing, caring for their animals, and their favorite thing of all, sitting by the fire as Father told his lavish tales. There were tales of dragons, griffins, knights, fair damsels, creatures, and even giants. Each girl sensed they were characters written in one of those tales. Father's tales resembled thrilling dreams and daring adventures. Theirs mimicked a nightmare from which they would never be woken. What the small group concluded would bring them joy and pleasure is also the same treasure so many have been consumed by—Sin, Lord Sin!

They would confront Sin with the intention of taking back their dear mother and father. Sophia possessed absolutely no doubt that it was indeed where they were. Why else would Father faintly whisper those words into her ear. Everything seemed uncertain from the very moment she sensed that cold touch of winter upon her nose that awoke her in bed—from making the choice to place her dainty toes on the frozen floor at their cottage to see what had caused the fire to extinguish. From that moment, what remains for certain is that she will not stop until she finds them. Unlike that flame back home, this fire within her will not burn out.

Savannah walked over to Sophia and brushed off a patch of dirt that was on the shoulder of her cape. "Are you all prepared, Soph?" Sophia looked down at her father's sword as she pulled it from her belt. Viewing the markings from her father's past encounters, she prayed that the same courage existed within her. She placed the sword back and brushed off the dust from her dress. "I have no choice but to have courage." She walked outside and joined her sisters as they congregated by the well.

Mrs. Wheat was overheard checking her husband as if he were a child about to depart for the schoolhouse. "Do ye got ya cleaning cloth? Do ye got ya snake butter? Do ye got ya flint?" He reassured her with "Aye do."

The old woman decided to ask the most important question regarding her husband's much-needed supplies. "What about your . . . your . . . your bloomas?" Augustus sprang up and threw his hand into the air while begging his wife to cease the embarrassment. "Tootie! Not in front of da lit'l angels. Dey don't need to be a hear'n about my a bloom'n bloomers!" Giggling was heard among them with even Ybbub joining in on the fun. The giant then said with the same high-pitched English accent as Tootie, "Oh yes, don't forget your bloomas, Mr. Wheat." Augustus turned to his old comrade and gave a look that would knock a beast to the ground.

Mr. Wheat, knowing that all the supplies had been accounted for, knew the most important part of leading an army was the mental preparation. After all, he was a former captain in the Royal Golden Eagle Army for many years. This was not his first assignment in locating evil and bidding to triumph over it, although it was his first in almost two decades. "Alright, my a lit'l angels . . . and Ybbub. Dis a place is about a two- or three-day journey from here. It's a not a gonna be easy. But if you a listen to a me and we stick a together, we will a make it. Rendben?" All responded, "Yes, agreed."

Tootie no longer could hold in her cries as she ran over to Mr. Wheat. Wrapping her arms around him tightly, she gave him a forceful kiss with great power and passion. Never had they seen what Father called a "smooch" with such magnitude. Sarah Honey's face turned blood red as she covered her eyes with her hands. Tootie wiped her lips and straightened her apron as a proud look cemented on her face. She was proud of her husband for the man he was but also fearful of the path they were about to embark on. She knew what that old knight of hers had accomplished and triumphed over in the past. She knew his abilities, skills, and unwavering determination that resided within him. At that moment standing there, the gray-headed, round-belly, wrinkle-faced man appeared just as young, brave, and handsome as ever to her.

Ybbub began kicking rocks while looking down at the ground. "Well, goodbye, sweet Tootie. I hope you're not still mad at me," he said in his low, grumbled, old Irish accent. The giant lifted his monstrous hand and waved goodbye while wiggling his fingers. Mrs. Wheat walked over to him, pulled his chin down by the beard, wrapped her arms around him, and laid a whopper of a kiss on him. Tootie's sworn enemy whom she had just pulverized not a day ago, was now receiving one of if not the most prized possessions a man could wish for—a kiss from a lovely lady.

She then slapped his round, rosy cheek as she looked him square in the eye and said, "You better take good care of my Augustus, Ybbub!"

With his face as red as an apple, Ybbub stuttered due to the shock and enjoyment of the kiss. "Aye, uh, my dear Tootie! Don't ya worry about that. I will indeed. Indeed!" Augustus was as surprised as Ybbub, not because his dear wife smooched another man but because he was flabbergasted that Tootie would be so kind to do so.

Mr. Wheat removed his leather arming cap and bowed his head. "May da good a Lord above a bless us and a keep us. Amen!" All replied in agreement. "Amen!" Mr. Wheat turned and placed his arming cap back on his head as he concluded his sixth and final check. "Time to a go!" As they entered the path, Augustus led the way, followed by Sophia, Savannah, Sarah Honey, and Ybbub, who brought up the rear—not just metaphorically. He held the reins to Gus who carried the weight of all their supplies. But the weight of guilt was upon Mr. Wheat's shoulders, the guilt of knowing the end of the path they were now on.

"Wait! Wait! Augustus!" Tootie yelled from the cottage door. She rushed inside momentarily and then quickly ran toward the group. "Augustus, here. Ya forgot this. Ya may need 'em dear." It was his old helmet and an iron chest plate covered in dents and scrapes, overlaid in gold matching the helmet. Mr. Wheat proudly took them. They observed this broken old knight don the armor of the Royal Golden Eagle Army. As the helmet sat perfectly upon his head, the same could not be said about the chest plate. As Tootie tried to tighten the leather straps, she continued to order her husband. "Augustus, suck in ya gut! Suck it in!" Finally, she was able to secure the leather straps to accommodate years of her delicious baking. Thanks to the old woman, the brave knight was ready to lead his army into battle, just as he did so many years ago sporting the same armor. Tootie ran back to the cottage as she took her apron and began wiping the tears from her eyes. As she looked down, she noticed the pale-yellow butterfly Savannah Gene had given her. That made her cry the more as the ones she loved began to fade into the distance of the Black Ghost Forest.

With the line formed in what one would view as the most unorthodox army ever assembled, the old knight observed his army. Girls all under the innocent age of eighteen and a quisby giant—a quisby giant he had known for almost four decades that was leading his no-good stubborn donkey, Gus. *Aye yi yi!* he thought to himself. *Dis is da worst a army aye have ever seen. No cavalry, no lances, no archers, no catapults, not even one trumpet or drum.*

Mr. Wheat turned and looked at Sophia as she followed behind him. She gave him a sweet smile of gratitude. Seeing her through the eyes of his helmet, he gave her a reassuring wink and turned back around. It was true, he did not have all those things as he did in the past, but what he had now was worth so much more. He now had a purpose—a purpose to help these little girls find their dear mother and father. A call was given to protect, and a call was answered. After all, he was a Protector of the Pure and an Avenger to the Wicked.

Chapter Fifteen

A Dead Ghost Haunts No More

A sharp, frigid breeze continued to gust through the massive monstrous trees, swaying high up to the heavens. Rays of sunlight pierced through the branches as a needle would fabric. There was the sound of the howling wind and the clanging of the cookware and occasional banter of old Gus. Heehaw! Heehaw! Ybbub quickly rubbed the donkey's head between the ears. "Shhh! It's alright, fella. Keep ya wits about ya." It was a sight indeed to behold—an 8 foot mammoth comforting a donkey through the Black Ghost Forest.

Mr. Wheat scanned the forefront as far as he could see due to the heavy fog that now smothered the forest floor. Still donning his prized helmet, his gray hair began to fade a darker shade as the sweat continued to roll down the back of his neck. His moustache protruded oddly just under the engraved eagle's beak while his round gut overlapped his worn and tethered belt. Tucked inside the belt, positioned at the middle of his back, was a silver-hilted dagger just smaller than the length of a short sword. Mr. Wheat's physical image fell short of the lean and intimidating nature that one would imagine a valiant warrior to possess. Standing at about 6 feet and generously weighing 280 pounds, this old man would have been mistaken for the group's cook, not their guide and experienced captain. Thankfully for Sophia and her sisters, the outward appearance is not what justifies or declares one a true warrior. Just observing how he maneuvered through the forest with each vigilant step as he watched and listened was a glaring sign that this old knight had been through a thing or two.

The girls, though, were still oblivious to the danger that withheld itself while they continued to navigate through the forbidden forest. They were wrapped tightly with quilts, their woven sacks were filled with scrumptious food, and their capes dragged on the muddy ground. Those blunt kitchen knives sat snugly in their belts.

"Be quiet, Scarlett," Savannah whispered as Scarlett proceeded to stick her tongue out in displeasure. The terrain had now become rocky and difficult as they followed Mr. Wheat. Tripping and stumbling over debris due to the poor visibility from the fog, they could not even see their feet as they looked down to the ground. A mystical mist blanketed their path, almost as if conjured by someone or something who wished to delay them.

After several painful days, the girls finally arrived at the heart of this terrible, mysterious place. Mr. Wheat suddenly stopped as he held his hand up in the air with fist tightly closed. Everyone stood still with not a peep or sound, including Gus. The old knight scanned the horizon as he gradually reached for his weapon of choice. He unwrapped the cold, steel chain from his leather holder as the iron spiked ball tumbled to the ground. An intimidating source of defense it was. He firmly gripped the leatherbound wooden handle as the linked chain led way to that menacing spiked ball. It showed no signs of being used for harm, but its purpose was to bludgeon the poor recipient with every swing.

Augustus turned to the left and then to the right. Beads of sweat dripped from the golden eagle's beak. Something was afoot, and their captain sensed it. He quietly motioned for the group to rally toward him. A circle was formed without a word as he positioned Scarlett, Sarah, and Savannah in the middle. Their defense consisted of a lazy giant, an old out-of-shape knight, and their eldest sister, Sophia. They were all they had now. This was it. Just the six of them.

The girls all felt nervous and fearful due to the uncertainty of what danger may be approaching. The sudden snap of a twig then echoed in the air. Mr. Wheat raised his head toward the treetops and whispered, "Draw swords." He was giving orders as if he were atop his steed years ago at the frontlines, leading thousands of the Royal Golden Eagle

Army. Each of the girls withdrew their blunt kitchen knives while possessing no knowledge of how to rightly wield them. Sophia firmly grasped her father's sword as her breath, now visible, bounced off the sharp iron blade. Ybbub, with fists clinched, lifted them to his bearded chin as a brawler conducts business in a tavern.

A blast of wind blew from above their heads as a black figure emerged from the treetops. Soaring over them as a vulture, its wings flapped as the wind gusted violently around them. It appeared to measure 12 feet from tip to tip, a massive and dreadful view indeed. With a sudden swoosh and quake of the ground, the fowl beast now presented itself before them as its wings blanketed its head and body. All they could see were the black, miserable, veiny wings that hosted scars as if they were markings sketched on a map—markings that led to no desired destination. They were features like hair-raising bats that fill the humid summer night's air.

A shout of "Leave us, beast!" then rang from inside the golden helm Mr. Wheat wore as he boldly stood with mace in hand. A smooth, deceptive voice laughed underneath the still-hidden wings. A gruesome noise uttered underneath—click! click! click! —like one's tongue snapping behind their teeth.

"Show yarself, ya mongrel!" Ybbub demanded in anger as spit flew from his large, chapped lips. "The sickening purity of your souls have festered a stench in my forest. I devour those who dare enter my dwelling."

The fowl beast slowly arose up from under its wings.

"I am Belzk." Fangs like daggers filled its mouth while two horns painfully came from its head, surrounded by thick, long, black, matted hair. There were claws at the end of its wings with hands as large as Ybbub's. A tail like that of a lion swayed as it stared at each of them with its yellow-infected gaze.

As the beast fully stood, its legs appeared strong and planted like a fierce lion. A wardrobe assembled by many unfortunate fallen knights' tunics bearing their coat of arms draped about his scarred body. Blood-stained-covered yellows, blues, and whites were all stitched and woven in the torn seams. Never had they seen a creature like the one who stood before them. Sarah Honey, hiding behind the lovable giant, began to whimper as she hid her eyes and tucked deeply into Ybbub's thigh. Belzk tilted his head to the side as it focused its attention on the little girl in the middle of the circle. A disgusting grin emerged from its face as he proclaimed, "Fragile as the egg of a robin."

Mr. Wheat stepped back, closing in the defense, and shouted, "Are you da Black Ghost dat haunts dis forest?"

Belzk bellowed a loathsome laugh. "If the Black Ghost is what has caused you to fear, then let it be so." Click! Click! Click! The creature crept closer toward them just as a lion circles its prey. In its mind, these despicable beings were the next victims that the village would never again see or dare to enter the forest to find.

"Now that's close enough there, ya rotten banshee!" Ybbub snarled as Belzk slowly continued to tiptoe around them. It was surveying the defense for a slight misjudgment so the weakest could be snatched as a field mouse in the night. Sophia could not comprehend what exactly her eyes beheld. A monster? A creature? A demon? What was this dreadful being? She held her father's sword, tightly gripping the hilt fashioned as an eagle's body. The wings, the hilts, ascended upward on each side of the blade. The pummel extending far past her small, soft, cold hands. It was all she had to distance herself from this winged fowl.

Click! Click! Click! Belzk continued to mock as its claws began to spread, each finger preparing to hand out a horrible fate. There was a sudden swipe, striking swiftly as Augustus profoundly ducked.

"Here! Here!" Ybbub shouted again in anger. Gus frantically attempted to jerk free and run. Heehaw! Heehaw! Heehaw! Savannah held the rope with all her might. Mr. Wheat stayed silent and focused as Belzk grinned while playing with his food. Ybbub, with fists still clutched and trying his absolute best to comfort the angels behind him, held his ground as he nervously mumbled, "Watch ya self, Augustus!" Another swipe! This time Sophia was the chosen prey. As she fell back, dodging the razor-sharp claws, she foolishly let go of her father's blade as it tumbled to the ground in front of the winged creature.

Black and gray was his cursed skin, and his yellow, bloodshot eyes were fixated on the precious treasure. The afternoon prey was no longer Belzk's concern as the clicking sound from his throat declared another hunger—lust to covet what Sophia had unintentionally let go. Belzk's black hair blew in the air as he slithered down to retrieve the sword that hopelessly lay along the forest floor. Mr. Wheat was poised as sweat profusely dripped from underneath his helmet. He calmly awaited the perfect opportunity to strike as a venomous cobra. The demon smiled while he knelt to retrieve the sword. Without thinking of the consequences, Sophia crawled and grabbed the blade with her hands. "No! Give it back!" she shouted as the creature began to slowly pull it from her grip, slicing her hand as she attempted to prevent him from seizing it. Blood began to pour from her hands as Belzk laughed at her failed attempt to triumph over his power. Sophia could no longer hold on as the sting of the sword sliced through her grip.

The old Captain knew this was the precise moment to attack. With Belzk's attention now cemented on Sophia, Augustus lifted the mace from the ground and violently swung it over his head. Belzk rapidly tried to steer clear as the strike broke a horn from atop his head. The forceful blow continued as the impact pinned his right wing to the ground like a meteor falling from the heavens. Screeching in torment, the beast vigorously tried to pull his wing free from the mace. Still pinned, Belzk swiftly delivered a forceful kick to Ybbub's stomach as it knocked him backward several feet over the three trembling girls.

Augustus pursued once more as he rushed toward Belzk's bloodied head and withdrew the dagger behind his back. Without hesitation, Mr. Wheat lifted the dagger high in the air with both hands, giving no attention to his injured arm from the previous battle. Belzk let loose an abysmal growl as his final fate stared him in the eyes. As Sophia watched, the old knight thrust the blade into the back of the evil soul. A roar bellowed from the creature as he fell limp to the ground, his claws digging into the bloody forest floor. "Too many innocent souls have dis a torturous beast a haunted!" Augustus shouted. Whether this was the true ghost that dwelled within the Black Ghost Forest or not, the trifling beast known as Belzk was no more. "Dis a ghost shall a haunt no longer! Da souls who once wore des tunics have been avenged by a my hands!" Avenged by an old Captain of the Royal Golden Eagle Army, a Protector of the Pure and Avenger to the Wicked.

Chapter Sixteen

The Heavy Toll Battle Takes

With bloody hands, Sophia crawled to the deceased foe that Mr. Wheat had slain. Even with lacerations deep into her soft palms, she grabbed her father's sword and clung to it ever so tightly. In her mind, she thought how close the dark creature had come to wielding her father's token of bravery and fearlessness. In her pain and suffering, she held the sword as tears began to roll down her muddied cheek.

With the traumatic event over, Sophia's emotions melted just as the snow on her body. The three sisters ran to her, providing what comfort they could. Savannah ripped her dress and used the cloth for bandages to wrap her sister's hands. Scarlett and Sarah Honey hugged her dearly.

Ybbub dusted himself off and walked to Mr. Wheat while leading Gus by the rope. "Ya alright there, ol' fella? What a nasty bludgeon that was ya gave 'em there!" he encouragingly whispered. Augustus stood there, showing no emotion. Breathing heavily while looking down at the lifeless creature called Belzk, he removed his helmet. As sweat ran down his face, he held his helmet in one hand and suddenly spat onto the demon's corpse. Augustus pulled the dagger from its body and wiped the blood from the blade with his cleaning cloth. Bending down, he cut the sewn tunics from the creature's body, rolled it up, and held it out to Ybbub. "We will a be takin dis, Ybbub." Mr. Wheat broke his stare from the beast and noticed Sophia sitting on the ground being comforted by her sisters. He stepped over the beast and shuffled to her after retrieving his weapons.

Kneeling beside her, he set his helmet at her feet. "In des a times, ya got a no time to a tink. It is a either turn and a run . . . or a charge and a fight. It a will not a be my a blood that dey are a wiping off a der blade." Mr. Wheat placed his hand under Sophia's chin and gently raised her head up while looking into her blue, tear-filled eyes. "Ya did a good, my lit'l angel. Yur a father would a be very proud." Giving her a wink, Augustus then gave her a kiss on top of her little head. He rose to his feet and helped Sophia up as well. Taking his rag, he wiped off her father's blade and handed it back to her. This was a symbolic ritual of the old knight that he had practiced for many years. It signified that past battles are no longer to be dwelled on. It meant to never question what had taken place but only to learn from it and use it to overcome the next adversary that chose to stand in his way.

Ybbub assisted the younger three girls, making sure they were as well as they could be considering the circumstances. “Come my lit’l angels. I think it’s time we had us a lit’l snack, aye?” He removed a handful of cookies from his pouch and stuffed them all in his mouth. Attempting to make light of their traumatic experience, he turned toward them with a mouthful of cookies and said with crumbs flying everywhere, “Um surry, did ya raunt srom crookies?” They all laughed and momentarily forgot the horrible experience they had just gone through. *Well done*, Ybbub thought in his mind, pleased to be able to create laughter in such a dreadful time.

“Aye, a we better get a moving, Ybbub,” Mr. Wheat insisted. “Aye don’t imagine it will a be long fur dem to come a lookin fur him.

“Renbend, Augustus. Better be a movin’ on aye suppose,” Ybbub agreed.

Mr. Wheat wiped the sweat from his brow and placed the helmet back on his head. “Stay a close and keep yur eyes a open. Aye don’t a tink dat is da only ting we got to a worry about in dis forest.”

Scarlett walked over to Ybbub and patted the donkey on the head. “Come on now, Gus. No time to waste. Right, Ybbub?”

Ybbub smiled and said, "Right ya are, Scarlett. Don't wanna be too far behind now, do we?" He yanked the rope attached to the old donkey.

Onward they went, traveling as if the recent skirmish had never happened. For these four girls, conflict would be unquestionably present if they continued pursuing their ultimate desire to find their mother and father. Sophia began to doubt herself with each step she took. "Was that who took them? What if Belzk knew where they were? What if they never find them now because he's dead?" Questions and doubt overwhelmed Sophia's mind the farther they went.

They walked and climbed over rocks and fallen trees as they cut through the thick brush to push as far as they could before nightfall. A grueling expedition they were partaking in had one requirement—faith. It required faith to push themselves and each other to their destination—Olcnom. After narrowly overcoming the obstacles already laid before them, it seemed now that just to take the very next step required an enormous amount of faith.

One marvelous thing was occurring, though, in the depths of such a horrendous mission. A bond was forming among them all, a woven, knitted bond as they began to truly depend on one another. Sophia looked at her blood-stained, bandaged hands and glanced back at her sisters. Behind them, Ybbub smiled, showing all six of his teeth. Turning back around, Sophia suddenly felt a peace come about her. Ybbub was right, Sophia thought. "Under the shadow of each other, people do survive."

Upon trotting through the forest for several miles, Scarlett could no longer contain her frustration and fatigue. "Does this stink'n place ever end? Or does it just go on and on and on and on?"

Continuing to push forward, Mr. Wheat replied, "Aye it does. Dis a forest will be da easiest part, aye am afraid to a say."

Scarlett sighed while kicking a pile of sticks as she passed by. "Well that's just great. We almost got eaten in a haunted forest, and we're not even close to being out of here yet." Savannah corrected her sister by just raising her finger to her lips, gesturing her to be quiet.

The elevation seemed to rise the farther they went, with the ground drastically changing beneath their feet. Bulky holes and chunks of sediment and soil looked like they had been disturbed by hundreds of wild rooting boars inside the forest. "What caused that?" asked Sarah Honey as she continued to walk while holding Savannah's hand.

Ybbub, noticing the sunlight had begun to fade, felt it was possibly time to settle down. "Um . . . Augustus. Don't ya suppose that these lit'l lasses have gone far enough today? Their wee lit'l tootsies have got ta be aching. I know mine sure are." Mr. Wheat stopped and placed his hands on his hips as his belly bounced underneath the armor while breathing heavily.

"Yes, I'm tired and ready for a nap," Scarlett said as she rubbed her belly., "And I'm hungry. Anyone got more cookies or monkey pudding?" Savannah walked toward Scarlett and reached for her bag tucked inside her belt. Noticing it was empty, she shouted, "Scarlett! You ate all your food! Why did you do that? Mrs. Wheat told you not to!" Scarlett jerked the empty bag out of her sister's hand, threw it at her feet, and shouted, "Because I was hungry! That's why!" Savannah, who rarely was unable to control her temper, showed no signs of bridling her tongue. "Why I oughta . . ."

Sophia jumped in between her sisters and separated them. "Enough!" Everyone stood perfectly still as Ybbub, Mr. Wheat, and Sarah watched in anticipation, awaiting a possible full brawel or wrestling match between Scarlett and Savannah.

"I'll bet two cookies on Scarlett," whispered Ybbub to Mr. Wheat.

"Not another word out of any of you!" Sophia reached down in her bag and shoved a handful of treats into Scarlett's chest with a look of dissatisfaction. Turning to Savannah, she sternly instructed, "Get your tent fixed and help your sisters with theirs after your finished!" Savannah curled her lip but bit her tongue as she walked away without saying a word, retrieving her bedding from the back of old Gus.

Mr. Wheat and Ybbub looked at each other, feeling the heavy strain of tension between the little angels. Mr. Wheat spoke. "Aye uh, yes, aye tink dis is a good a spot to a make camp. Don't ya believe a so, Ybbub?"

Ybbub quickly agreed, swaying his large arms back and forth as he clapped them together. "Grand—a grand spot indeed. Nice and cozy, aye."

Sophia retrieved her bedding from Gus's back and began to prepare her own site. Throwing the stakes, canvas, and blankets on the ground, she leaned her back against a large oak tree. Smoothly sliding down its trunk, she allowed it to gently guide her to the ground. She folded her arms and placed her head down to conceal herself from the neighboring annoyance.

After Augustus finished assisting Ybbub with the other tents, he walked over to where Sophia sat. He removed his helmet and sat down along the base of the tree with her. The sun was almost completely hidden, and the last bit of light had faded behind the treetops. Quietly the old knight whispered, "Ya know, aye can't a hardly eat a just one of dem cookies." He patted his armor-covered, round belly. "And a don't a get me about dat a monkey pudd'n."

Sophia lifted her head. Mr. Wheat could see the tears streaming down her cheeks. "Do you really think we can find them, Mr. Wheat?"

As she wiped the tears with her cloak, he stretched his arm out and tapped her on the knee. "Ya know, notin' in a life is a certain. All ya can a do some a times is . . . a just believe. Look around ya, lit'l angel. We are all a here because a we believe. We a believe dat we will a find dem, and ya know a what?"

Sophia wiped her nose as she replied, "What?"

The old knight continued. "Aye believe in a yu too. Just a like aye a did a yur a father." Sophia smiled and rested her head on his shoulder. "Yur a precious lit'l angel, ya know dat? What a wonderful bunch of a lit'l lasses yur rotten father has."

Sophia raised up as she again wiped the tears from her cheek and asked, "Do you have any children, Mr. Wheat?" He sat silent with his gaze cast upon the helmet beside him.

Ybbub suddenly walked over while dusting the dirt off his knees. "I'll be back shortly. I'm gonna go and gather some wood for . . ."

Mr. Wheat sprung up from the ground and interrupted Ybbub mid-sentence. "No! No! Aye a will get da firewood, Ybbub. You stay with da lit'l angels." He scurried into the forest, picking up branches and limbs and placing them under his arm. Gus, desiring to follow, began whining. Heehaw! Heehaw! Heehaw! "Aye yi yi. Shut up, you a useless beast! You and a Tootie never a hush!" Mr. Wheat was heard shouting in the distance.

Ybbub began laying out stones in a circle to prepare for the campfire. "That's a fine fella there. A grouchy one, but a fine one indeed." The large stones appeared to be pebbles while clutched in the behemoth's grasp.

"Ybbub, do Mr. and Mrs. Wheat have any children?" Sophia asked quietly. The bear-skin-covered giant halted in his tracks. With arms full of stones, he let out a dreadful sigh from his chapped lips and turned his back toward Sophia. As she beheld him standing there, she could see the simple inquiry regarding the Wheats' household had turned into an inquisition of some sort. "Ybbub?" she whispered.

His round dirty face was now an easel, harboring a canvas painted with shades of distress and grief. Wishing the young lady had not inquired about such things, he still felt the sweltering desire to reveal the truth to her.

Ybbub turned and knelt as he began to carefully place the stones in a tightly fit circle. "Aye uh . . . Aye don't think that it's my place to be jabberin' about such things."

Sophia leaned toward him. "Ybbub, please! Why is that such a difficult question? I want to know."

Ybbub stroked his brown beard and threw a handful of twigs into the center of the ring. He scanned the wood line and hoped he would not regret the choice he was about to make. "Ceart go leor," he mumbled under his breath. "I'll tell ya the story. But it is not a grand one at that. Not a grand one at all."

Chapter Seventeen

A Knight's Terrible Tale

With the night sky settled in and the calm breeze dancing atop the flames, Ybbub proceeded to answer Sophia's question. "They uh . . . had a son . . . and a daughter."

Sophia squinted her brows in confusion. "Had? Where are they?"

The giant unenthusiastically allowed the dark, mournful topic to spill out in their midst. "That's quite a tale, my lit'l angel." Ybbub glanced over as Augustus's helmet caught his eye. Memories and thoughts he had attempted to erase had now begun to bubble inside him, resembling a disgusting bog within his mind.

"What happened to them?" Sophia whispered.

Ybbub continued. "Years ago, the grand evil that resides

in this world began to fester. It grew, spreading its cancer to the edge of all that is wonderful and pleasant. Thousands were taken, captured, and drawn to its shininess. Many kingdoms fell to their wicked hands. But one—one kingdom stood up to it, refusing to take another step backward. A line of shields, swords, and brave souls were made to push back—to push back the spread of Ri Sin and attempt to get back the loved ones they had lost."

Sophia interrupted him, "The Righteous Kingdom! The Royal Golden Eagle Army! Right?"

Ybbub nodded his barrel-sized head. "Aye! The Kingdom sent all the bravest and fearless warriors they could for the purpose of smashin' such evil. Sent to confront Ri Sin, these knights and soldiers marched adorned in their gold armor to meet him at his door. Augustus, your father Daniel, and Mr. Wheat's son Regal—they marched to Sin's door."

Sophia's eyes opened wide as the name ran familiar to the family's trusty, dependable Clydesdale—the horse that Father spent so many evenings in conversation with and adored.

"They met the putrid wolves of Sin and fought bravely they did. Them three were on the front lines as they led this final clash. As the armies collided, Ri Sin slashed his way toward them, slaughtering Logan, the Great King of the Righteous Kingdom who stood in his path. The Great King gave his life he did for what he thought was most important, his people. A great a man he was at that. Ri Sin towered before them as he raised his flaming sword above his head. As the blade began to fall, your father charged him alone, blocking the fiery sword that would have led Augustus and Regal to their doom."

The unexpected rattle of wood and twigs beat off the ground and startled Ybbub and Sophia. "Oh! Augustus, ya startled me! Didn't know ya were back there." Ybbub and Sophia remained silent as they watched Mr. Wheat strike the flint taken from his pocket along the moss and twigs in frustration. The flash of the red and orange sparks cast a glow about the old man's face as it showcased the apparent obviousness that he had been standing there the whole time, listening. The dry twigs and leaves caught fire as his chest plate lit up like a street of gold.

"Go on. Tell her da rest," Mr. Wheat mumbled while breaking twigs and throwing them carelessly into the fire. No one said a word. Savannah, Scarlett, and Sarah were all fast asleep, snug in their blankets and huddled together in one tent. They were exhausted from the many miles they had covered on foot in the Black Ghost Forest.

Augustus unbuckled the leather straps to his chest plates and set them to the side. Taking his hand, he brushed his white moustache and rubbed his bloodshot eyes. "Aye a yur father, he charged dat devil. Aye a saw da flaming sword a coming right a to me and my a son. Aye a could feel da heat smolder against my armor as it got closer. His eyes burned as if a filled with brimstone as he a stood der with a one a purpose. Da purpose to end all dat is a good."

Sophia looked at Ybbub as he continued to stare at Augustus. "What happened?" she nervously asked.

"Aye a yur a father saved my life. Everyone a watched as a Daniel charged dat devil and blocked Sin's flaming blade with his a shield. Da devilish beast's sword cut through as it a sliced into his left arm."

Thoughts of Father's scar that he carried on his arm came to Sophia's mind. Never had he explained the origins of how he received it.

"Shaken dat he possessed such bravery, Ri Sin den a grabbed Daniel by a da throat and a lifted him off da ground. As he squeezed and stared deep into yur a father's soul, Daniel beat and struck him with all his strength lika a cat dat had caught da tail of a mouse. It was a useless. As da life began to a leave yur father's body, my a son Regal took his sword and cut da hand that laid hold to Daniel's throat. Yur a father fell to da ground as Regal stood before Ri Sin. Aye watched in disbelief, frozen from what my eyes a saw. Ri Sin swung his sword as da flames a burned ever so brightly. As smoldering ash a falls from da mountains, da blade . . . uh . . ." Augustus began to choke while his eyes overran with tears. He placed his hand over his mouth.

The grief that he bore was far more than what Sophia could have imagined. It had been years since this old man had spoken about such a horrific account. Knights in the past often loved to brag and measure their bravery among each other but not stories such as these. These tales and accounts are much preferred to be placed in a grave and deeply covered, never to be cited, heard of, or told again.

The old man was finally able to regain control as he decided to continue. "He fell. Da flames cut right a through my son. All dat aye could a do was a watch. Aye couldn't move. Couldn't speak. Couldn't breathe. Aye uh . . . aye a saw my son, my a lit'l boy. Lifeless. He a sacrificed himself fur a me and a fur yur father. All dat is a good in dis a world."

Sophia felt broken by the horrible truth and was overcome with sympathy for the old man as she began to cry. "I'm so sorry, Mr. Wheat." The old man nodded his head up and down gently.

"Daniel rose to a his feet with da blood pouring from his a cut and broken arm. He took dat a very sword and rammed it into da chest of Ri Sin, chipping da end of da blade. Da devil pulled back and a roared as a lion. He and his army fled. At a dat moment, Sin felt he had a been defeated but vowed to return. A terrible storm of fire and ash a exploded from a inside his kingdom as it a began to rain down a on top of us. Der was a yelling and a screaming as we all tried to escape the fire dat rained down from above. Yur a father grabbed me and a drug me back to da forest, da very forest we are a in now. We all a ran for our lives as a some were . . . some were a not so fortunate. Aye marched with a five thousand soldiers. Aye was der Captain. But a only a few returned. Dat was da last time aye saw a Regal." Augustus then broke down as his head fell into the palms of his calloused and blistered hands. "Dat was da last time aye saw a my lit'l boy."

Ybbub stood to his feet. “Ya did good, Augustus. Ya served them men well. Aye know that’s a hard for ya. An old dog for a hard road, aye,” Ybbub said as he leaned over and patted his dear friend on the back. Sophia looked down as the hilt of her father’s sword glowed from the flames of the campfire. Placing herself there years ago, she began to feel troubled for Mr. Wheat but ever so proud of her dear father. Questions she had struggled with all these years had now been answered from the words of an old knight’s terrible tale.

Mr. Wheat went on. “Aye, it ‘twas a horrible a time for me and my a dear Mrs. Wheat. First our lit’l angel and den Regal.” He felt a sudden gentle hand on his shoulder from behind.

“What happened to your daughter, Mr. Wheat?” It was Sarah Honey who had snuck out of the tent while he was telling his difficult revelation. Sophia wanted to deter her youngest sister from asking more questions but at the same time deeply desired to know his daughter’s fate as well.

“Sarah, no! Hush!” Sophia frantically stood up trying to shoo her back to bed as if she were a lamb that had escaped its pen.

“Connie . . . dat was a her name,” Mr. Wheat said as he threw another log on the fire. “Aye a told her to stay away from dis a forest. Aye always caught her at a its edge, peeking and a feeding to its a mystery. Den a one day, her friends said she a finally just a stepped in, no longer a able to fight, it’s a draw. Dat was da last time anyone ever a saw her. Dey ran and a told me dat she walked right in. Several of us went into da Black Ghost Forest to look for her. Da King even sent his knights and many of a my men to help me try to a find her." The old man shook his head while staring into the fire. "Just a baby. Sweet and innocent. Twelve years old and a still our lit'l angel."

"But Mr. Wheat, you live in this forest, don't you?" asked Sarah Honey.

"Aye," Augustus quietly responded. "I've spent a many years a looking for her, a hoping dat if she maybe a come back from its a depth, she would find a our home. Find a me and a her mother. Aye a miss Connie's sweet lit'l a face."

The group all felt the immense remorse and pitiful sorrow that Augustus had kept locked up inside, just as he did with his helmet, tucking it away. He hid it within himself, hoping the last two decades were a nightmare—a nightmare that he prayed earnestly to be awakened from. As the fire continued to devour the charred, cindered logs before them, so too did the haunting reality beneath the old knight's armor. It never ceased torturing his soul.

Chapter Eighteen

Stampeding Herd of the Stagnus Tree

Sophia tossed and turned all through the cold, bitter night, even with the warm, crackling fire providing some welcome comfort. Exhausted from the excruciating journey, she knew now that its effects had begun to take a toll on her. She was consumed with so many wonders about what Mr. Wheat had sadly spoken of—the sacrifices, friendships, battle, and loss of his two dear children. The fearlessness that her father possessed and the bravery that Regal honorably exemplified played in her mind. Now more than anything, the grim truth she wished to know but greatly feared was finding out what happened to little Connie.

Lying there pondering all this in her heart, Sophia clung to her father's sword. With her hands still sore, wounded, and bound from denying Belzk from claiming it, the sword now meant more to her than ever before. It was a reminder of her dear father's fearlessness and Regal's bravery. At last, her mind began to settle as she drifted off to sleep.

It felt as if as soon as she closed her eyes, Savannah was shaking her shoulder. "Sophia. Wake up." The tinkering and clanging of pots and pans further assisted her sister's soft voice in waking her up.

"Come on! Ya better get some of this grub before it's all gone. Aye can't promise there will be any left for ya now," cheerfully stated Ybbub while sitting on the ground cooking breakfast with a tiny fork and pan atop the fire. Tootie had packed a generous amount of food that Ybbub had already made himself familiar with. "What'll ya have, my lit'l angel?" he asked Sophia.

"Sausage and flat cakes will do," she said while stretching and letting out a yawn.

Mr. Wheat advised across the campsite, "If a you would only have as a much a passion for a fighting as a ya do stuff'n yur a face, Ybbub, ya would be more useful." Already dressed in his armor and packed up, Mr. Wheat had finished his last spoonful of monkey pudding.

"Augustus, my dear friend, giants are like bagpipes. Nothing good comes from them until they are full!" Ybbub joyfully laughed as he engulfed a stack of flat cakes in his large mouth.

Mr. Wheat rolled his eyes. "Aye. Yur a full of a sometin'," the grumpy old man mumbled as he walked back over to Gus, disgusted. Scarlett sat there with breakfast smeared all over her face as she carefully listened to Ybbub's wisdom.

"My lit'l angel. These cookies are most wonderful and delicious when lightly roasted." He carefully placed the cookie in the pan for a few seconds and then quickly pulled it out. He began to hand the warm cookie to Scarlett but paused for a moment. Breaking it in half, he generously gave her the smaller portion of the two. "Don't want to eat too much now, do we?"

The girls watched as they noticed Mr. Wheat standing on a fallen tree near Gus. He proceeded to remove a feather from his pocket and hold it out in front of him. "What's he doing?" asked Savannah while finishing her last bite of sausage.

"Why, he's check'n the wind, of course, seeing how much farther we've got ta go," Ybbub replied.

Augustus released the feather from his hand as it drifted roughly three paces in front of him. "Aye! Not a much a farther, Ybbub. About a day's journey," he said while staring up at the sky. "Dat is if a we get a movin!" Mr. Wheat picked the feather up from the ground and placed it back in his pocket. "Alright a me lit'l angels. We a better get a movin.' Ybbub, put dat fire out. Gus is a itch'n ta go." Ybbub, appearing disappointed that breakfast was over, mumbled his old Gaelic language under his breath and smothered the fire.

Savannah thoroughly checked her two younger sisters as Sophia had instructed her to do. The quilts they had been wearing for the journey were now tightly packed on the back of old Gus. The air felt as if it had become much warmer than the day before. She believed their cloaks would do for now. "At least the snow had held off another day," Savannah said.

Mr. Wheat formed the line again as if he were back leading his army into battle. "Alright, a it's Sophia, Scarlett, Sarah, Savannah and a den it's da dumb giant. Dat will do. Stay close." Augustus placed his helmet on his head, clutched the leather-wrapped wooden handle of his mace, and pushed forward.

As they walked, Sophia felt she had a better understanding of what some called a crusade. After listening to Mr. Wheat, the idea of him risking his life to help them find her mother and father did not come with such guilt. Maybe Mr. Wheat needed them just as much as they needed the old knight. He, too, had a loved one who, if found, would satisfy his soul. She agonized, though, supposing she might have to wait many years just as the Wheats had in which no answer had come. Sophia realized she had to do just as Mr. Wheat told her the night before—believe.

The forest seemed to be never-ending to the four young lasses. Such a gloomy and grim setting displayed a reality of torture. They all walked, climbed, and hiked for miles through the forest. One's mind begins to play tricks in these types of travail. "Are there any more of those scary things? Ya know, like Belzk in here?" Sarah Honey asked Ybbub as he nervously bit his bottom lip,

"I'm not sure. But if there are, I'll pound 'em and break their wings apart. I'll . . . I'll snap off their horns and use their claws to pick out the meat from my teeth!" The giant, obviously joking, instantly made Sarah Honey's fear fade away. Ybbub always seemed to make light of every situation no matter how treacherous or dim.

Mr. Wheat thought as they pushed through about how incredible the four little angels were. He had served with many brave knights, but these four angels were some of the most daring individuals he'd ever accompanied. They wore no armor, carried no shields, rode no valiant steeds, and had absolutely no experience in warfare. What they did have, though, was determination. *Remarkable des a lit'l lasses are*, he thought in his mind. *Da tings dey have already a conquered.*

The sun began to shine brighter as midday came. Eating as they walked to cover as much ground as they could, Ybbub thought of a merry idea. "Oh my! Aye've got a grand ceol for ya lit'l darlins!" he shouted.

"Ceol?" Savannah asked.

"Yes, my sweet Savannah Gene. A wee lit'l tune for ya. A melody!" Ybbub joyfully sang while leading Gus behind him.

Fee . . . fi . . . fo . . . fum.
Aye hear the sound of their beating drums.
Be he far or be he close,
I'll tear off his ears and eat it on my toast!
In my grasp I'll rip off his legs,

Dash a lit'l salt and mix it with me eggs!
He'll be lying there, scared and shaken
I'll throw 'em on the skillet
And cook 'em with bacon!

Ybbub let out a boisterous hoot as the girls followed with their high-pitched giggles. "Dats enough der, Ybbub," Mr. Wheat said without exhibiting a smile beneath his gilded helmet. A rattling boom echoed in the sky. He believed it to be thunder.

"That's odd. I don't see any clouds," Scarlett said as they all looked up toward the heavens. "It doesn't appear as if it's going to rain," Savannah said while gazing above.

The ground began to violently shake as if an earthquake had started to tremor beneath them. Mr. Wheat slightly raised his helmet up as a tender breeze blew through his white moustache. His eyes widened, and a nervous gulp from his throat thumped. "Dat is a not a rain, me lit'l angels." Boom! A deafening crack resembling thunder sounded once more. The ground quaked as they all nearly fell to the ground.

"What's going on?" shouted Scarlett while clinging to Ybbub and trying to keep her balance. A rapid gust of wind blew toward them, nearly knocking them back to the ground. The old knight stood to his feet and then pointed as he screamed, "Aye yi yi. Stagnus Trees! Run!"

All six rose to their feet and scrambled through the wreckage, trying to keep up with Mr. Wheat. While running,

Sophia could not believe what was occurring. Another fairy tale she had heard all her life had come to fruition before her very eyes. The wind ghastly blew through the forest sending limbs, branches, and leaves into the air. "Follow me!" shouted Mr. Wheat as they all dodged the objects while struggling to stay close.

"Over there!" Sarah screamed while pointing at an enormous oak tree as it began to rip its roots from beneath the ground. The snapping of the roots was ear-splitting as they splintered from deep within the ground. Let it be known that this was not inflicted by a mere storm or natural disaster. This was a result of something far unnatural. That is simply because the trees were moving. "Quick! Hide here!" They all rushed to a cluster of boulders along the hillside. As they ran, Sarah Honey became frozen in her tracks. With her cape flowing in the wind, her eyes beheld several immense living trees stampeding at her. Unable to move the slightest muscle, she squealed in terror.

Ybbub, releasing Gus's reins, leaped to her as the tree was about to use her frail body as planting soil. The heroic giant scooped her up like a kitten and tucked her underneath his arm as he rolled out of the way. A rooted foot slammed down while dropping clumps of dirt and grass on top of his head. The giant lunged over the boulders where the others nervously watched. Once again the quisby, lazy, good-for-nothing giant honorably showed chivalry and heroism. Those were his thoughts, of course, as he clung to the mud-covered little angel.

Out of harm's way, the young ladies observed the greatest majestic scene their eyes had ever beheld. It is believed that more than most have been blessed to witness the transformation of the vibrant leaves as autumn sneaks in and quickly vanishes into the bitter tones of winter. Such enchanting pigments fill one's eyes of the turning in such a marvelous way. This turning was none that these innocent eyes had ever viewed.

Yes, the forest was changing, but this did not require the moving of the sun, changing temperatures, or the lasting light of the glowing moon. Instantly, the depths of the Black Ghost Forest were clearing before them. *How is this possible?* the girls thought as each peeked above the rough, jagged stones they depended on to provide a somewhat secluded protection. Echoes of shuddering voices sounded as if the mountains were crashing round about them. Even Mr. Wheat, who had witnessed such things before, was in awe. No matter if one had witnessed it before, to understand such magic is never comprehended. It can only be appreciated and respected.

Sophia turned to Savannah with leaves stuck in her hair and said with a smile, "Baby Gene, the girls at the village will never believe this. Stagnus Trees!" Both wore smiles while delightfully watching the marvelous display no one would ever believe. Yet again, Father was telling the truth the whole time.

Louder the roars grew as they covered their ears to keep from busting the drums inside. Mr. Wheat hastily threw his helmet off as the ringing vibration filled the inside of it like a bell joyfully ringing atop a chapel. A few moments later, the trees finally ceased the destruction and chaos. Many of the lifeless trees remained in place while the Stagnus Trees appeared to have migrated for better soil, water, or sunlight. They move for reasons mortal man has not brought to light yet. No explanation can be given. It was another jaw-dropping tale that only those who were there to witness would ever believe to be true. It was a tale all six no doubt would remember for the rest of their lives—the day they witnessed the great moving herd of Stagnus Trees.

Chapter Nineteen

A Few Hundred Knights in Misery

Relieved the Stagnus Trees had migrated on and thankful the chaos had stopped, Mr. Wheat rose from behind the boulder. "Aha!" he shouted while placing his helmet back over his arming cap.

"What is it, Mr. Wheat?" asked Scarlett while looking up at the old man standing on the boulder. He resembled a captain as if he were on the bow of a ship venturing across the seas.

With hands on his hips, the old knight looked down and stated, "Aye, my a dear. We've almost a made it through. Just a one more path, and den dat should a be it." All smiled, including Ybbub as they began to feel the reward for all the hardships they had endured up to that moment. It was a pleasant sight, Mr. Wheat thought, to behold them all joyfully celebrating. If they only truly knew what that last stretch inhabited, they would not be so gleeful. He feared what they must endure to reach their ultimate destination.

"Come along," he said while performing another self-check. "We can't afford to a lose anymore a sunlight." Each climbed over the top of the boulder as they brushed off the debris from their clothes and hair. With a swift glance over the line, Sophia checked her sisters to make sure their provisions and supplies were all accounted for. While they all withdrew a small snack from their woven bags, they knew the drill at this point of the voyage. There was no time for dining while being filled with lavish stories and delicious food. Each second spent could result in a fatal conclusion. Lunch, snacks, and dinner must be consumed on the go as time was of the essence. The same constant thought played like a harp in Sophia's heart—the safety and well-being of her mother and father. Each day, hour, minute, and second could cost them dearly.

The little ladies were all ready to go, while still waiting on Ybbub. He had started feeding Gus his sack of oats. Not keen on concealing his temptation for taste, the giant's beard became littered with sprinkles of oats. "Ybbub, are you eating the donkey's oats?" asked Savannah.

The big giant stood there hunched over with his back turned. With a muffled mouth full of dry oats he mumbled, "Nhhooo. Rye?" Oats were then seen falling as snowflakes from his mouth down to his bearskin-covered feet. Sarah laughed once again at her now hero.

"Aye yi yi. Let's a get goin'," Mr. Wheat said as they all viewed an unfamiliar scene. Scattered boulders now filled the forest floor while smooth large stones were stacked atop one another. Trees oddly placed periodically in their midst created a difficult obstacle to safely cross through. The thick forest timber had morphed into a different landscape than they had become accustomed to.

The sun had begun once again to dwindle to their disadvantage as they all carefully followed Mr. Wheat. The forest terrain began to change, evolving into a slightly elevated ascent. Thick, heavy grass grew alongside the boulders as the wind constantly seemed to blow in this portion of the Black Ghost Forest. It could be compared to the warm breeze just before a midsummer's storm, the kind that carried an eerie feeling, sending a tingle down one's spine knowing that nothing courteous would follow its presence. As they all felt this tingle, they continued to navigate on through.

A fowl was spotted in the sky above as it flew swiftly over them. "Oh no! Not again!" shouted Scarlett as she frantically ran to Ybbub.

"Aye, uh wait a just a minute." Augustus tilted his head as he squinted though the eye holes of that golden helmet. "Aye yes! A blessing a from up above aye! Dats a my falcon, Solyom!" The bird hovered over as Mr. Wheat whistled and raised his arm. The falcon descended gracefully and gently landed on his forearm. Comfortably balanced, the bird tapped the forehead of Mr. Wheat's helmet as if it were greeting him with a kiss. A large bird with a broad wingspan, it was intimidating as it stared at each of the young onlookers. Its sleek feathers were made up of brown and sandy shades along its upper body and streaks of the same throughout its underparts with pale underwings. Solyom's piercing call was as sharp as his curved talons that tightly gripped its master's forearm.

"Why aye am a happy as a monkey dats found its tail!" shouted Mr. Wheat.

"That's your falcon?" asked Sophia as she stretched out her hand to greet the magnificent creature.

"Aye, he's a saker. Der is none better, aye Ybbub?" he pridefully boasted.

"Aye, Augustus," Ybbub agreed. "That bird is quite the hunter, lit'l angels. He's a good lad that Solyom is. Augustus has had 'im for about what? Twenty year or so?"

Mr. Wheat nodded his head while admiring his old friend. "Aye, and a good help a he will be to us. He must of a not a been able to see us 'til dos trees moved, ya know. Aye sure am a glad he did. Let's get a goin.' Hold on, Solyom," Mr. Wheat continued as Ybbub gave a cheerful snicker and led Gus along the trail. Even with the arrival of Augustus's weapon of old, this falconry would be no match for the evil beyond these boulders.

After they had walked for about an hour, the sun cradled the mountain's edge, making their shadows grow stronger. "Sssshhhh! What was that?" Sophia whispered as they all stopped. The hair on their necks raised, standing straight up due to the clatter in the distance. The sounds of a bullhorn, haunting moans, and shrilling yells were all followed by a devilish laugh. Instantly the jolting gallop of a horse raced by them. "What in heavens was that?" whispered Sophia. A gruesome sight appeared before their very eyes—knights clad in armor bearing swords, shields, flags, and lances. Several dashed along the small, worn path the six were now guilty of trespassing on. For a second time, another brushed by as the ghostly figures harbored no ill will toward them. Spirits! Ghosts! Ghouls! All frightening but hypnotizing shades of violet, lavender, and amethyst. Illustrating a radiant glow within the chilling dark setting of the Black Ghost Forest, these soldiers ran and marched about as if nothing in their presence mattered. One gave a stern order that appeared to bestow a tilted crown atop his chain mill head.

Lift the banners.
Draw your swords.
May we fight to the death
Defending our lords!

Dead they were, and alive they were. The dead quickened at the stroke of nightfall for the objective of waging war. Just as placing a mirror in front of a mirror, so too did these troubled souls view their tortured eternity with no demise in sight. It was a harrowing image full of tearful sadness and dooming heartache. Their moans and screams played like a band in sorrowful procession. Parading the spiritual chains, they felt ever so tight about their spirits. These dubs of old were at a spiritual standstill while bound in the cursed, forsaken forest—the Black Ghost Forest.

As they formed flanks and dressed the lines, the six quickly ran from one boulder to the next, attempting to not get in the way. Several rushed by jousting atop their steeds, while others fought in their presence, clanging against the armor. It was a sight of incomparable proportions. These ghosts were not used to having an audience of the living in their presence. The command rang out again, louder than before.

Lift the banners.
Draw your swords.
May we fight to the death
Defending our lords!

Mr. Wheat was overcome with guilt and empathy for them as he watched in awe. He knew of the grisly tales concerning the lost knights chained inside the Black Ghost Forest. Stories had spread throughout the Righteous Kingdom with fears that would pierce even the bravest of knight's armor. The Knights of the Broken Wing—soldiers stranded inside the perpetual forest, cursed from a conflict of old forgotten days. They were a conflict of legend and brokenness consumed by grief laid upon them long ago. Wedged in the confines of this wooded prison, their lone enemy to which they harmed was indeed themselves.

The count of the poor souls was unable to be recorded. Incapable to justly claim an exact number of shields and warriors, a safe projection could be written and sealed with wax to a few hundred. A few hundred miserable, violet, lavender, and amethyst glowing souls striking and bashing as the hues of colors danced undesirably, intertwined with the fog that crept along the forest floor. They continued to do what they died perfecting—the state of war, but with each other.

Sneaking by, the girls held hands while desperately clinging to Ybbub. Poor Gus was drug about by the giant who himself was glazed with spook and fright. No matter who you were, this was no scene of pleasure and contentment. Heehaw! Heehaw! Heehaw! Gus had tripped over a mound of rocks, instantly casting attention on the group. The army of ghosts fixated their distress on them. All had ceased, holding their weapons and banners that blew violently in the warm breeze. The crowned warrior slowly directed his horse to their location. Staring at them for but a moment, he let out a shout.

Lift the banners.
Draw your swords.
May we fight to the death
Defending our lords!

The opposing sides re-formed and joined flanks as they marched in their direction. With their weaponry displayed and presenting intention to spoil, Augustus laid hold on Sophia and shouted, "Run! Up da hillside der!" All immediately darted to the hillside as it drastically ascended to a rough, jagged top.

"Hurry! They're getting closer!" shouted Ybbub while trying to scurry everyone up the hill. As the army shaded in violet and amethyst perused them, the group felt as if their doom had finally caught up with them. The crowned knight galloped as he jolted for Ybbub. Just as he pulled his sword from his scabbard, the miserable soul stopped. Silence drenched the warm, thick air as the ghostly souls looked on them. The tilted crowned knight raised his sword as the horn sounded yet again. The order echoed into the night like a hopeless leaf drifting about a rough rivertop.

Lift the banners.
Draw your swords.
May we fight to the death
Defending our lords!

With all breathing heavily, Mr. Wheat placed his fist on his chest. Appearing to honorably salute those forsaken warriors, he clanged two thumps on his breastplate. Sophia watched as the sheer knights began to fade while marching back into the Black Ghost Forest. "What are they?" she asked. As Augustus consoled Solyom who was perched on his master's shoulder, he sorrowfully uttered a whisper from inside his helmet. "Miserable. Dey are miserable."

Chapter Twenty

The Battlefield of Misery

Olcnom—just meditating on what evil that festers such a kingdom could in no way draw one's desire to view its dastardly makings. Yet these six souls were on the edge of that very empire. Remarkably they now followed a worn dirt path up the rocky hill. It is a true oddity that such a trodden road could lead to a destination of pure wickedness. Heavy was the weight of eeriness upon each of the four girls. Feelings of raw maliciousness and anxiety draped over them like the heavy pack on Gus. With each step, Sophia grew nervous to think what could reside on the other side of the mountain.

Up the hill they went as pots and kettles clanged. The feeling of exhaustion became more alarming than the tinkering of the cast iron. "The night sky seems to be light'n up there, Augustus!" noted Ybbub.

Knowing it was well past sundown but not yet morning, Mr. Wheat said, "Aye tink we are a just about der."

Ybbub raised his nose toward the heavens and gave a sniff. "Smoke, Augustus. Uh, awful stench that is."

Mr. Wheat stopped and lifted his helmet as he whipped the sweat and dirt about his face. "Of course ya do." He then removed the feather from his pocket, held it about his face, and released it. Straight to the ground it fell with no drift or gentle glide.

Solyom let out a call while nervously flapping his wings. Thick smoke filled the air as the night sky began to be engulfed with flashes of fire and lightning. The gray clouds were not calmly drifting about like the ones the girls had once gazed at with their mother. These were circling violently above in a wide circumference that stretched far throughout the sky. Lightning bolted up above as thunder boomed, shaking the ground. "Aye yi yi. We are a here," said Augustus.

Sarah Honey jumped as the boisterous echo startled her. Clinging ever so tightly to Ybbub, she longed to be anywhere but there. Already the kingdom had sewn fear into all their little hearts' fabric. Sophia grew fearful as she knew they had not even viewed the Kingdom, yet it was already an intimidating realm of horror.

"Stay a low," Mr. Wheat warned. "Just a over dis hill and we will see it."

Ybbub cradled Sarah and Scarlett as they all cautiously crawled to the top of the rocky, jagged hill. "It's alright, my dearies. You're safe with ol' Ybbub," he whispered. Mr.

Wheat turned and motioned with his hand for all to stay put. As he eased up over the jagged edge, the glow of the Kingdom beat against his gold helmet. The engraved eagle turned bright red as the smoke, fire, and lightning shaded its beauty. He then motioned for them to rise and see it for themselves. Anxiously, they slowly arose and peeked, finally observing what they desired most—Olcnom.

A vast desolate field with marshes and bogs scattered before them, bubbling in spots as brew in a cauldron. Thick, deadly smoke polluted the precious air and led to a remorseful sight. No gates. No defense. No guards. Nothing like any other kingdom they'd ever seen or heard tales about. "I don't see anything. Nothing to keep us from getting in," Sophia said.

Mr. Wheat quickly responded while continuing to monitor the field. "Aye, for a what reason would one have a to come to such a wicked place? Dey have a no reason to keep anyone a out. Nobody a would dare try and enter in der."

Sophia then said as she firmly held her father's sword, "We are."

Ybbub then gave a playful grin and winked at Augustus. "No doubt thaaat's Daniel's daughter there for certain."

In the far distance they could see a sizable castle that resided underneath the circling clouds full of fire and lightning. Buzzards and fowl creatures flew, scanning the field for undoubtedly their next victim or meal. "What are those white branches scattered down there?" asked Savannah. "I don't see any trees."

Ybbub looked at the group and whispered, "Those aren't branches, lit'l angels. Those be skeletons."

What they saw lying about were unmarked memorials of sadly forgotten displays of courage and bravery. Those were the skeletons of fallen warriors who had lain in the bowels of Olcnom for ages. Augustus turned around and slumped to the ground. Confused, they watched the old knight battle something within himself. Unknown to them, the heartless field that lay before them was the same abyss where his son, Regal, had bravely fallen to Ri Sin's blade. It was the same field where he had witnessed the notable campaign many years ago, where he led those mighty knights of the Royal Golden Eagle Army to their doom—so he had unwaveringly thought all those years later. The wretched guilt he carried was accompanied by shame. He could not blot this burden out of his mind, no matter how valiant a knight was dubbed or perceived. After all the triumphs, victories, and conquests, it 'tis the one he failed that lingers utmost in his memory.

"What is this place?" asked Savannah with her eyes open wide, showing the fear smoldering inside her soul.

Mr. Wheat placed his hand about her shoulder and said, "Dat's da Battlefield of Misery."

Sophia was still sitting there with the horrible thoughts of her mother and father being chained, tortured, or worse within the walls of the castle. She spoke up. "What's the plan?"

Ybbub turned to Mr. Wheat as well, waiting for orders from the old Captain. A silent pause. "We find a your mother and father. Follow me."

Scarlett stood up as she broke away from Ybbub and angrily interrupted. "Oh, so I guess we just stroll on through the marshes, walk underneath the flying whatevers, and go knock on the castle door? Tell 'em we've come for our mother and father? That's it, huh?"

Augustus casually responded, "Aye. Dat's a it. You got a better idea?" Scarlett's mouth dropped as she stood looking at Sophia. "Renbend! Follow me."

Mr. Wheat and the group walked back down the mountain to the left of the field. Flashes of lightning and blasts of thunder continued to decimate their poor eyes and ears. "We a gotta cut down da edge of dis a mountainside. It's a deadly drop a down, so be a careful and a quiet." He walked over to Gus, the old good-for-nothing donkey of his, and said, "Aye believe dat dis is a far enough fur you, old a boy." He patted his head between the ears while removing various items from the pack. He distributed extra food, water, and candles to his little army. The most odd and peculiar occurrence then took place. Mr. Wheat cupped his mouth with his hand and whispered softly into the donkey's long, outstretched ear. Gus gave a sudden nod as he shook his head up and down, turned about, and began walking back from whence they came.

"You can't just let him go into the forest by himself," Savannah said loudly.

"Oh, he'll be alright, me lit'l angels," Ybbub assured them. "He's a bit stubborn at times, but ol' Gus is smarter than what ya think. Ain't that right, Mr. Wheat?" Ybbub smiled as he took a handful of cookies and shoved them roughly into his mouth. While staring at his old friend trot away, he mumbled, "Aye. Dat he is."

The old knight looked over the group and began to instruct them. "Tighten yur a belts and yur a boots." He walked over a ways from them to check his own supplies. Augustus then removed his weapon of choice as he swirled it over his head. A swooshing chain whisked about as the spiked ball violently circled over him in the air. The girls curiously watched as he removed the dagger tucked behind his back and felt the edge with his fingers. After preparing his dagger and mace, he carefully withdrew a crimson piece of ribbon about the size of one's forearm from his leather buttoned pouch. The old man bowed his head for a moment, mumbled a few words, kissed the ribbon, and gracefully secured it back inside the leather pouch attached to his belt. It was almost as if this were a pre-battle ritual he had become accustomed to throughout his long, trying years of service—a ritual to prepare one's mind and focus.

Sarah Honey, only the age of ten, asked him aloud, "What's that crimson ribbon for, Mr. Wheat?"

Solyom flapped his wings while still holding onto his master's shoulder. Augustus quietly responded and then walked over to Sarah Honey and patted her on the head. "Dat's a just a memory, lit'l angel."

Sophia once again checked her sisters just as she had done before. She inspected them all one by one to make certain they were all equipped for the final stretch. In her heart she was worried that even though the Battlefield of Misery appeared unoccupied and desolate, there still resided an evil presence there. “I hope Gus is okay,” Savannah said as Sophia looked over her. “He’ll be fine,” Sophia said. “Now keep Sarah close to you, and don’t let go of her hand.” Focused and more than ready, the oldest was, although she still lugged the unbearable burden all the way from their tiny, happy home to the outer realm of Olcnom.

They were all prepared now to receive their next orders from Mr. Wheat as they stood before him. “Take a yur time. Get yur a footing and don’t a slip. Dat’s a long a time to a wave goodbye aye.” He was the first to embark on the terrorizing pathway, attempting to blaze the trail for his fellow friends. As he led the way down the mountain, all followed behind. Rough and rocky was the mountainside as it gave way with each step. One slip or misjudgment could be fatal.

Farther they descended as the fowl flew high above them as if waiting for one poor, unfortunate soul to certainly make a mistake that would lead to the horrible pit of misery. Ybbub was last in line since the sight of a towering 600 pound giant scaling a slippery cliffside is in no way comforting or pleasant.

A sudden crack of thunder roared above, causing Scarlett to immediately slip. Several rocks let loose, rapidly rolling down the side of the cliff. “Savannah! Look out!” Tumbling vigorously, one rock struck Savannah in the head, knocking her unconscious. Her grip let go of the mountainside as she fell backward.

"Augustus!" shouted Ybbub. Mr. Wheat swiftly lunged to catch Savannah as her fingers slipped through his calloused, muddy hands. All watched in horror as she fell to the bottom of the mountain and disappeared from sight. Thankfully, her fall was aided by a small cluster of brush at the foot of the mountain in the bubbling marshes.

They all frantically scaled down the mountain while shouting for Savannah. "Savannah! Savannah!" No response. Mr. Wheat lifted Solyom up in the air with his arm as the saker flew directly down to where Savannah had fallen. Solyom's distinct call could be heard as its master knew no contact had been made yet. "Hurry! We gotta get a down der to her." Dust and rocks blanketed the cliffside as their hearts raced, fearful of what they might see at the bottom.

"She must of fell at least 100 feet," shouted Scarlett while trying to assist Sarah down the hill.

"Savannah! Savannah! Were almost a der," Augustus said. Fearing the worst, they finally reached the brushy area. Mr. Wheat withdrew his dagger as he sifted through the brush. Ybbub laid hold of Scarlett and Sarah as Sophia took out her father's sword.

"Savannah! Answer me," Sophia screamed as they all sank up to their knees in the swampy marsh. Cutting through the brush, they pushed through, hoping to locate poor Baby Gene. That's what Mother and Father had called her since she was a baby. Memories of her sister flashed in her mind like the lightning and fire above. Since Sophia was two years old, she and Savannah had been best friends. Seventeen years later, it had all led to this moment.

"Der! A trail!" Mr. Wheat located a muddy trail as if something had been dragged through the marsh. He heard a call from Solyom in the surrounding area. "Quick! Follow me!" he shouted from underneath his helmet. Briars, thorns, and thistles pulled but failed to hinder them as they tore through. "Savannah! Savannah!" Suddenly, they heard a deadly scream. "This way!" shouted Sophia as they rushed to the left of the heavy, thick terrain.

Taking her father's sword, Sophia made a final cut, giving an open view of the field of Misery. There she saw a tall creature donning a torn, raggedy cloak dragging Savannah by the leg as she screamed and begged for aid. "Savannah!" Sophia and Augustus shouted as they ran toward the figure. Sophia tripped over a cluster of bones in the marsh as her foot sunk to the bog floor. Mr. Wheat, unaware, continued running to the creature as Savannah scratched and clawed the ground to free herself.

"Unhand her, you a rotten maggot!" Augustus shouted as the creature calmly continued its course. Ybbub and the others assisted Sophia out of the bog, lifting her up out of the strong suctioned mud. Her shoe sank into its depths as she became free. With one shoe, Sophia and the others frantically ran behind Mr. Wheat. Closing in on the malefactor, Ybbub removed a leather strap from his deep pocket and a small stone. The giant quickly placed the stone inside the leather strap and began to twirl it over his head. Swish! Swish! Swish! Swish! Swoosh! Like the crack of a bullwhip, the strap shot out the smooth stone. Smack! A direct hit from the slingshot. (Quite ironic if you think about it. An 8 foot, 600 pound giant's artillery of choice—a leather slingshot.)

"What a volley! Did ya see thaaaat?" Ybbub said aloud. Echoes of "Well done, Ybbub!" paraded inside his large head. It was very impressive, but the stone had now seemed to anger the creature instead of hindering it. Savannah's captor had come to a halt while she remained a prisoner in its clutches. Mr. Wheat carefully walked toward her as the beast rumbled a disturbing growl. The hair on the back of the old knight's neck raised due to the sound that resembled a ravenous wolf. The beast slowly turned around and faced Mr. Wheat. "Aye yi yi!" Mr. Wheat fearfully mumbled under his breath as he saw what exactly hid beneath the hooded cloak. The beast had a long, pointy snout, a snarled mouth full of razor-sharp teeth drizzling with foam, and eyes as yellow as the burning sun.

As it stood up on two legs, Mr. Wheat knew now exactly what it was—a Verfarka! Known to some as a wolfman, the beast stood there as its snarl grew to a roaring chomp. Smack! Ybbub delivered another strike with his slingshot, the stone busting the Verfarka right in the snout. "Did ya see thaaat?" Ybbub bragged. "Come on now! Is anyone else seeing this?" The beast violently began shaking its head in pain as its attention was diverted from Savannah. Lying helplessly on the ground while the foam and drool dripped all over her, Savannah had a sudden idea. Her kitchen knife! The Verfarka's nose continued to drip with blood as Savanah withdrew her mother's dull kitchen knife from her belt. As the beast snorted and panted, she thrust the blade into the beast's foot! A grisly roar resonated in the marshy open field. The deadly grasp that the fur-covered beast held on her leg was now let loose. Savannah was able to crawl to Mr. Wheat as she hid behind the old knight with mace in hand. The Verfarka bent down and removed the blood-covered blade with its teeth. Raising back up, the creature gave a vibrating howl toward the sky. Ybbub, Scarlett, Sarah, and Sophia gathered behind Mr. Wheat, not knowing what might happen next.

The bogs filled with thick steam as they bubbled and exploded with awful gases into the dense air. Mud burst from the wet ground all around them. Hands and arms sprang from beneath while the terrifying sight of bones and graves encamping about added fuel to the fire of their kindled fright. Decomposing knights and warriors of long ago had somehow instantaneously received life from the bellow howling of the werewolf. Skeletons! The grim Beo Creatlaches wretchedly pulled themselves from beneath the water as the dead became the living before their very eyes.

In the meadow, clans of repugnant hobgoblins hunched as they shuffled from their concealment, harboring clubs. As the ghouls crept in, the group huddled into a circle with their backs against each other, finding themselves encircled in the once-desolate field.

"No wonder they call this the Battlefield of Misery," whispered Sarah Honey. Mr. Wheat began to look around as he noticed a blue wooden shield bearing a white antlered deer as its coat of arms. He swiftly bent down and pulled the shield from the dark, thick peat and firmly grasped it with his left hand. With his mace in the other, the old knight was more than ready for whatever foe stepped before him.

Sophia withdrew her father's sword once again as the bubbling wickedness approached. Just the six of them now held the line against the dead living and foul creatures of Ri Sin's kingdom. The excruciating journey had led them to this unpleasant place, to their possible unprofitable death on the Battlefield of Misery. The Verfarka howled once more into the smoke-filled air as he slowly crawled in their direction. Holding the gold-hilted sword, Sophia knew this was it. If the undesired reality of death was at the end of this vigorous journey, let it come. But it would not come without a fight.

Sarah began crying as the marsh burst, the lightning flashed, and fire smoldered above in the clouds. The decomposing knights, skeletons, and hobgoblins charged them. "Come on, ya bloody gan chroi! Ya filthy buggers!" Ybbub shouted as the giant was seemingly overcome with anger. In what felt an eternity, the mob rained in as thick hail.

"Ahhh!" Mr. Wheat swung his mace as it instantly delivered fatal blows to at least three of the Beo Creatlaches. Two of the hobgoblins grabbed hold of Ybbub from behind as he flung both of them clear across the field, treating them like a bear shaking off a pack of hunting dogs. "Ya want ta jig now, do ya?" The mammoth displayed a grand showing of strength.

One after another the inhibitors funneled in. Ybbub and Mr. Wheat had done well trying to keep all four girls safe, but unfortunately they began to feel overrun by their opposing army as they approached from every angle. "There are too many!" yelled Sophia. The little girls withdrew their small blades as they prepared for the worst in the new territory of combat. Only several days ago they were playing with dolls, braiding hair, and building snowmen. Now they were pursuing war and engaged in battle for their very lives.

Augustus fought valiantly, wielding the mace as an artist would a brush on a canvas. The old knight was as skillful and effective as he was twenty years before. Ironically, there were only two more days until the anniversary of that great battle twenty years ago, the great battle from which he carried the burden of such suffering and loss—the loss of his only son, Regal. He felt in his heart that now was the time to redeem himself. Refusing to be chained to the curse of guilt any longer, he did not wish to spend the rest of his days dubbed "the Knight of the Broken Wing."

The girls screamed in pure terror as Sophia stood there wielding her father's sword while the conflict happened before her very eyes. As the cramping, malodorous herds piled in, the words Mr. Wheat told her while sitting beside each other by the trunk of the tree rang in her mind. "There is no time to think," he had said. "Just fight! It must be done!" Would she be able to keep such courage of stone as Mr. Wheat or when it mattered most falter as the sand of the sea? That's what she feared most of all. Failure.

The sickening odor of blood, the chiming of bones snapping, and the piercing pitch of the screams all suffocated her ability to participate. Sophia frantically held her sisters close as they all watched in panic. The festering abominations of Olcnom began to swallow their hopes and try their faith of ever obtaining the goal they set out to accomplish. Now they were miserable in the Battlefield of Misery.

Chapter Twenty-One

The Greeter of Olcnom and the Blade of Despair

Lightning soared from the sky as the clouds engulfed with flames above. The group had maintained their line in a noble manner. How long they could maintained it was the harsh reality as Ri Sin's Kingdom exhibited no shortage regarding servants of darkness.

From the marshy, muddy field these servants sprang up, appearing to never cease. They lived with one purpose that beat in their dead, unrighteous hearts—to inflict misery. "Aye don't a tink we can a hold 'em much a longer!" shouted Mr. Wheat as he swung his mace and crushed the cranium of an oncoming living corpse. Solyom, no longer able to cling to his master, flew up out of the skirmish. Sophia yelled while huddling with her three sisters, "We have to head to the castle—to Mother and Father!"

While punching and kicking as if in a tavern brawl, Ybbub tripped over something on the ground. Falling back on his extremely large rear, he briskly sprang back up and noticed the cause of his stumble. He saw an old, worn chariot wheel, the culprit that had brought the giant down. Ybbub suddenly had a rare idea and rapidly rose to his feet, shoved several skeletons away, and yanked the chariot wheel from the marshy ground. The wheel was made of iron and wood, and its circumference was much wider than the giant. As he held it firmly, its height measured to his chest from the ground. "That'll do!" he yelled. "Augustus! Sophia! Everyone get behind me and stay close!" Ybbub held the sturdy iron wheel, gave an old Gaelic yell, and rammed through the oncoming defenses. Misery's inhibitors bounced off as the relentless barrage trampled over their foes.

The mobile battering ram charged the castle, breaking through Ri Sin's regional offense of spewing wickedness. The sound of their bodies, armor, and bones thumped and clanked as none could break Ybbub's stride. With bones, flesh, and ligaments flying in every direction, the charade resembled riding a horse through a field of daisies. The two youngest girls struggled to keep up with the fast-paced race to the castle of Olcnom. Augustus, seeing their decline, decided to slightly fall back and hold off the pursuing loathsome adversaries. As Augustus began to engage, an odd thought stumbled into his mind. "Aye wonder if dat donkey has made it yet." Thankfully, he returned to his senses and quickly ducked, missing a sure fatal blow from an approaching hobgoblin.

The withered knight was focused yet again as he endured to defend his tiny militia.

Savannah, continuing to stay with Ybbub, looked behind her and screamed. "He's coming!" The odious Verfarka had begun to dash dastardly on their trail. Refusing to leave with an empty stomach, he was now in pursuit of the fresh meat that ran behind the iron chariot wheel. Its growl could be heard, while his speed was unmatched with anything they had ever seen before. Dirt and moss flung in the air as its claws ripped into the soil. With the Verfarka's ears pinned back, fangs glaring in the firelight, and cloak waving in the wind, the small victory they claimed appeared to be short-lived. Verfarka speedily approached them—30 yards! 20 yards! 15! 10! Augustus closed his eyes as he awaited the horrible agony of being ripped apart by the beast.

Just as the beast began to pounce, something blew a blasting horn from within the castle. The chilling Verfarka stopped abruptly. Augustus opened one eye, peeking as the beast stood still, breathing heavily right before him within arm's reach. Confused while still holding the mace and shield, Augustus was not certain of the meaning of the horn. Nonetheless, he was surely grateful for its timing. Sophia and her sisters gathered around Ybbub as he tightly grasped the chariot wheel while breathing heavily.

Another quivering blow of the horn was initiated as the inhibitors of the Battlefield of Misery scattered to the marshy pits, frantically hurtling and plunging into the bubbling, steaming bogs. The Verfarka gave a menacing growl as it whimpered and rushed back to the secluded thicket where Savannah had previously fallen.

All stood in awe as they witnessed the battlefield deplete like a fire dwindles in a blizzard. Seeing the cohorts of evil scatter in panic, Sophia felt a sudden chill about her neck. Turning around she realized they were now at Olcnom's door—the door that leads to Sin, Ri Sin! Ruler and Lord of Olcnom!

As they turned around, a black, double-iron entrance suffocated their sight. Its stature ascended to the thick cloud of smoke above that ever circled the forsaken kingdom, a proclamation of eternal suffering. Even deep into night's slumber, the clashes of fire and lightning above catered a spotlight, illuminating the gestation nest of impurity. No torches or candles were required to see. The light of the Kingdom of Sin burned for the whole world to behold—to behold and fear.

The sudden sound of iron door hinges plucked a troublesome, terrible tune. The gates began to open as blankets of dust swallowed the group standing there helplessly. Screams and moans packed their ears as they echoed into the ashy air. The suffering voices of many escaped the iron fire of Ri Sin's realm as the vibrations bounced off Mr. Wheat's armor. The warm, humid air cut through their hair and faces, and they began to gather close to one another. They dreaded what horrid tribulation may be on the other side of the iron doors. Rumbling shouts blasted from inside, and drums beat deep within the heart of the kingdom as chants rolled with the force of a mountain crumbling. Chants of the forsaken tongue hearkened.

Dee La Dee La Volda Rashka Ri Sin!
Dee La Dee La Volda Rashka Ri Sin!
Dee La Dee La Volda Rashka Ri Sin!

These iron doors were not crafted lifetimes ago for the purpose of keeping the outside from coming in but to keep those that are in from going outside. "What are they saying?" asked Sophia with a trembling voice while huddling her three sisters.

Mr. Wheat, looking at the iron gates, replied, "Dey are a praising der king."

Through the crack between the two iron doors, they saw a black figure mounted on top of a steed. Donning a black tunic and armor covering its entire flesh, the figure's identity remained a lifeless secret. Trotting with each eerie step, the figure's horse was decorated with a black caparison in which it flowed in the piddling ashy wind. Approaching closer, they could only see the horse's bottom cannon. Bone. Only bone. The horse was that of no other. Only bones made up this evil figure's eho donned beneath the caparison fabric. The demon confidently and intimidatingly rode on top as it approached the group with no fear present in its bowels.

Ybbub glanced at Mr. Wheat. "Augustus, who by dragon is thaaat?" The old knight stayed silent as his eyes locked upon the black figure. The flames and the cracks of lightning grew more powerful as the entrance to Olcnom opened wide—wide to those who dare enter. The kingdom's greeter who halted before them was now their only obstacle from stepping in. It 'twas not an army that thwarted their entry but only a single foe. This must be a testament to the potency and confidence Ri Sin must have in this Greeter of Olcnom.

The castle's threshold lay just behind the figure as if it was a backdrop to a dreaded desire they sacrificed so much to reach. As the drums banged and the chants rang out, the greeter slowly lifted its hand, clanging its armor beneath the ripped tunic. Providing evidence of his tenure within the realm of Olcnom, it was blatant that no conflicts of defeat were recorded in its past. The chants and drums ceased as if the eyes of the kingdom resided on their greeter. The horse's eyes were red, troubled, and painful, bearing a soul trapped with destitution and misfortune of high degree.

They heard rattling beneath the horse's neck, which was a prideful display of human skulls bound by iron chains. The demon wore a helmet fashioned with iron like that of a bull. As it breathed, smoke violently blew from its nostrils as it ascended upward past the iron horns that pierced through the hooded tunic. Steam and water dripped from its snout as its devilish stare provided no relief to the group who stood before him trembling in fear.

The greeter slowly lowered its hand back to the reins of the horse while continuing not to utter a word. Mr. Wheat cautiously stepped forward while firmly gripping his mace.

"Aye am a Sir Augustus Philipe Wheat, Captain of da Royal Golden Eagle Army, Protector of da Pure and Avenger to da Wicked!" An instant roar belted vigorously from inside the kingdom— "Dee La Dee La Volda Rashka Ri Sin!"

The greeter then spoke in a low, terrible voice as if several souls spoke at once. "I have feasted upon your blood before." The devil removed a skull from its cloak, held it high into the air, and threw it in front of Mr. Wheat. It distastefully bounced along the ground while continuing to roll at the Captain's feet. The painful memory of long ago burned Augustus's mind. He knew in himself whose poor skull it was. "Regal!" Mr. Wheat's voice shuddered as rage sapped his emotions beneath the royal helmet. Ybbub quickly grabbed him as he began to lift his mace to deliver a retaliating strike with trembling arm. The old knight was consumed with madness as the hot blood fueled with vengeance flowed through his veins.

"No! Not now, Wheaty," the giant pled.

"Aye will avenge a my son! Aye will avenge him!" Augustus vehemently shouted as it bellowed from inside the helmet he wore.

The greeter slowly lifted its right hand once more and pointed his finger in the direction of Sophia. Her heart sank just as she did into the river of death with the skeletons days ago. "Fright and doubt blanket your soul," the greeter bellowed.

Ybbub carefully stepped back to the girls, continuing to face the greeter, "Here Here! Ya got no place jigg'n with these lit'l angels." Sophia's courage and bravery had seemingly been tested throughout the past trying days. Knowing she now stood in the same battlefield as her father did years ago, she knew being afraid was no longer an option. "I am not afraid!"

She stepped out from behind Ybbub, while Mr. Wheat and the giant both turned about, shocked to hear such words come from the little lass's mouth. The sound of drums thundered once more as each strike quickened the tempo of the dreadful cadence.

"I . . . I am Sophia. I've come for my mother and father!" The greeter's horse shook its head as its eyes blazed an ever-deeper red.

With the drums thumping inside, the greeter eagerly replied, "Your journey has been in vain. Six souls shall be laid upon Ri Sin's altar, all certain to be sacrificed for naught, for they have been slain by the High One."

"Liar!" Scarlett yelled, full of anger and frustration, overwhelmed with the same courage as her oldest sister as they now stood together before him. Only several paces separated them from the Greeter of Olcnom.

"Aye Dat is a true, my a lit'l angel," shouted Mr. Wheat. "Dis servant is a consumed with evil. Der is a no truth within dis empire. He is wormed with iniquity. Aye a believe a notin' dat proceeds from yur a jesting lips."

The greeter chillingly laughed as his knuckles clinched tightly around his horse's reins. "I prophecy death shall fall on you. Just as death choked your son and her father and mother." The greeter steered his horse away from them and turned back to the front doors of the castle. Paying them no attention any longer, he continued into the heart of Olcnom.

Mr. Wheat shouted violently, "Aye demand Daniel da Fearless and Noel da Sweet!" Echoes of the drums, chants of the praise, and the crash of lightning above shook the ground they all stood on.

Dee La Dee La Volda Rashka Ri Sin!
Dee La Dee La Volda Rashka Ri Sin!
Dee La Dee La Volda Rashka Ri Sin!
Dee La Dee La Volda Rashka Ri Sin!

"Mr. Wheat! What do we do?" Sophia shouted as she looked to him for instruction. As he looked at them all, he saw the physical embodiment of defeat. The old knight knew many years ago he had returned home empty-handed, haunted and terrorized all those years and unable to live a happy and peaceful life. Praying for one more chance to somehow avenge his son and find his lost little girl, Mr. Wheat turned to the greeter and began to follow him. "Aye am a not a returning home a empty-handed again!" He then rushed the path of the Greeter of Olcnom with mace and shield in hand. As he closed in, he began to swing the mace over his head, whipping through the ash and smoke with the spiked ball and chain. Time felt as if it stood still while memories of Regal and Connie flashed in his mind's eye as he swung the mace, not at the foe himself but into the eho he rode upon. The possessed horse crumbled to the ground as its bones snapped like a twig in the winter. The greeter fell helplessly off the saddle and onto the Battlefield of Misery.

The demon of Sin rose to its feet as he drew a blade from beneath his long, tattered tunic. As the sword slowly showed itself from the concealment of the sheath, its song was not to that of iron scraping iron but the sorrowful melody pitched with cries, pleas, and terrible begging screeching in endless torture.

Fumes thickly blew from the iron bull's nostrils as the greeter's armor clang with each step. Holding his sword, the greeter lifted it in front of its steaming nostrils. Mr. Wheat stood his ground as the figure towered over the old, weakened knight. Ybbub and the girls looked on, not knowing what could possibly occur next. Even fearing the worst, they all still reserved a glimmer of hope for their Captain who had led them to Olcnom's gate.

"Aye am a Sir Augustus Philipe Wheat, Captain of da Royal Golden Eagle Army, Protector of da Pure and Avenger to da Wicked! Aye demand Daniel da Fearless and Noel da Sweet!" Augustus firmly grasped his mace and shield. He had mastered both of them many years ago and devastatingly used them on the same field for the greater good. Swearing an oath to give his life to protect and his willingness to sacrifice it even if required at this moment, he watched patiently as the greeter moved closer to him. It raised its long claymore in the air, and the clouds thundered and fire engulfed the pillars of smoke. "May the Blade of Despair's thirst be quenched by your blood."

The Greeter of Olcnom swiftly slashed down as Augustus raised his shield. The force of the claymore knocked him back to the ground as he thankfully blocked its fatal strike. Augustus let loose his mace as he looked to his left and observed it was within arm's reach. He quickly reached to lay hold of the leather-bound handle when suddenly he felt a searing, burning sting. A warm and wet sensation overwhelmed his senses as he looked to his left. Gone! His left arm had been completely severed! As Augustus's pain set in, the greeter slowly and confidently walked on him as he lay wailing on the bloodied ground.

Hearing Mr. Wheat cry in agony, Sophia screamed, "Mr. Wheat!" Ybbub held her back as he froze stiff in the moment.

"You have failed once again," whispered the greeter as it lifted the blade high above its iron-horned sallet.

Augustus gazed up from the ground at his adversary while wincing in uncontrollable pain. Oddly, memories of him and Tootie sitting close to one another on cold winter nights by the fire drinking cocoa, playful days of roughhousing with Regal, and walks in the tulip fields with Connie were what he truly saw at that instant. A somewhat peaceful feeling saturated his broken spirit as he accepted his fate while lying in his own blood on the Battlefield of Misery.

Mr. Wheat closed his eyes and mumbled a prayer beneath his helmet. The slashing of the wind and the cries of countless souls taken by the Blade of Despair could be heard as the greeter began to deliver the final blow. Just as the sword came within inches of the old knight's head, from the sky above Solyom swooped in and struck the hilt of the claymore, letting out a glaring caw. As an arrow is fired from the string of a bow, so too was the swiftness of this Saker Falcon. Olcnom's greeter lifted its eyes up to the heavens to catch a glimpse of what had hindered his claim of another meaningless life. Solyom swooped in once more, this time from behind as the falcon violently struck the back of the iron bull helmet.

Mr. Wheat realized that this was the moment he had prayed for many years while living in the Black Ghost Forest. He struggled to rise to his feet as blood poured from his severed arm. Shuffling as quickly as he could, Augustus picked up his mace from the ground. As the greeter continued to try to push away Solyom, it was unaware that Mr. Wheat had risen to his feet. The old knight swung the spiked ball forcibly over his shoulder. He heard nothing but the sound of the chain rattle and the pounding of his beating heart. With one last twirl, the desperate father gave all he had left. Thump! The spiked ball, as if placed directly from the good Lord above, docked into the neck of the armored hound of Olcnom.

The greeter let loose his sword as it drifted helplessly from his fingers to his feet. Falling to his knees before Augustus, the greeter dauntingly blew smoke from his nostrils, fading with each second as all watched in astonishment behind Mr. Wheat. Solyom darted to the ground as it hastily picked up the greeter's sword and ascended back into the air. As Solyom soared just above its master, Mr. Wheat lifted his hand up as his falcon let loose of the blade. It fell perfectly into his grasp, and the old knight delivered one final blow to the greeter of Olcnom as the iron bull helmet toppled to the ground.

Augustus, numb from the loss of his arm, stared at his adversary's headless body that lay on the ground. The sword branded as the Blade of Despair had now been liberated from the armored demon known to this day as the Greeter of Olcnom.

Chapter Twenty-Two

A Cloak, a Courtroom, and a Door

Blood coated the blade in Augustus's hand, but it 'twas not just his own blood. Once again, the old Captain achieved the impossible while leading the little army to the entrance of Olcnom. Ybbub and the girls rushed to his aid as Savannah and the giant tightly wrapped bandages around his severed, blood-soaked shoulder. "Tootie's gonna kill me, Augustus. Absolutely gut me," Ybbub nervously mumbled.

As they finished fashioning his bandages, the iron doors suddenly began to close. Sophia yelled, "The doors! We've got to get inside!" Augustus placed his mace inside his belt and held tightly to the defeated foe's sword as Ybbub helped carry him. Each one followed Sophia as she ran with one shoe still missing to the closing entrance. All were fearful of the possibility that their last hope of rescuing their mother and father from Ri Sin's clutch could be closing as well. Sophia entered first, followed by Savannah, Sarah, and Scarlett. "Hurry! Hurry!" they all shouted as the door's opening creeped ever so near shutting. At the last second, Ybbub threw Augustus beyond the entrance and lunged inside just behind him.

The entrance slammed shut, causing the earth to tremor and shake. Soot and cobwebs fell from the inside on their heads. It was pitch black with no ability to see even their hands in front of their faces. Smothered in darkness and uncertainty, they had finally made it to the destination of their quest—the realm of Olcnom, the castle of Ri Sin.

The trickling of dripping water and the aroma of a spoiled hog carcass held their senses as they all huddled together, unable to see a thing. "Anyone got a candle handy?" whispered Ybbub.

Sarah Honey felt around in her small satchel. "I do!" Ybbub retrieved two pieces of flint from his leather belt pouch and struck them together. The flash of sparks lit the room each time as they disturbingly saw briefly within the flicks where they now dwelt. The candle lit up as Ybbub carefully held it with his hefty fingers. Good enough was the small flame as they observed the grand hewn stone walls around them. That torturous dripping of what was believed to be water was in fact not water but the shrill sound of dripping blood.

Abruptly along each side of the walls, torches instantaneously immersed with the most unusual flames they had ever seen. Pigments of emerald, jade, and lime danced in the iron sconces overhead that led to a twisted stone hallway. "Aye guess dats where we a need to go," uttered Augustus who was in terrible pain.

As they slowly crept up the hallway, they heard disturbing moans and screams in the castle. Augustus no longer led the way as the agonizing intense pain flirted with his consciousness. Continuing to still hold the trophy he had won against his foe, he had now begun to use it as his walking staff.

"Sophia, where are we going?" asked Scarlett as they all blindly followed her up the spiral hallway. After walking continuously for several minutes, they finally reached the top.

An open courtroom with pillars and stone slabs lined in rows encompassed all the desolate chamber. Torn and raggedy banners hung from the ceiling timbers as they waved from the cool, damp draft that blew inside. As they continued to walk, Savannah whispered, "What is this place? Why isn't there anyone here? Is the castle empty?"

Augustus replied while leaning on the claymore. "No, my a lit'l angel. Not a empty at all." Passing by the stone blocks they could see skeletons resting in various armor of great kings, knights, and warriors of old, each from countries and kingdoms near and far as they lay clinging to their arms of warfare. Long swords, rapiers, falchions, halberds, spadones, and even a battle axe all bore the poor brave names that had fallen to the wicked hand of Sin.

"Look, Augustus!" shouted Ybbub. "King Logan the Meek!" The once noble monarch from years ago clung to his arming sword while still dressed in his armor. Viewed while lying on the stone block was the truth regarding his imposing default—a smoldered puncture located in his chest plate, signifying the king's ultimate end. In his hands was a beautiful masterpiece indeed, forged from iron collected from the depths of Golgrathia. Bound with brown leather tightly fashioned around the hilt as the pommel, guard, and blade shined like a mirroring crystal sea.

"Aye yi yi," Augustus whispered as he and Ybbub stared at the legendary sword of the once-adored humble king. The chants were then heard from inside the castle, vibrating through the thick stone walls.

Dee La Dee La Volda Rashka Ri Sin!
Dee La Dee La Volda Rashka Ri Sin!

"There's the drums again," Scarlett said as she stepped closer to the giant.

"Don't you worry. Old Uncle Ybbub ain't gonna let nothing happen to his lit'l brawler."

As Savannah and Sarah continued to scan the room and read the names chiseled into the stone blocks, they read a familiar name aloud. "Sir Daniel Th . . . Sophia!" Sophia then ran across the room to her two sisters as she saw with her own blue eyes the name of her father etched in stone. "Father's name! Mr. Wheat! Ybbub, look!" They rushed to her as they all viewed the mystifying puzzle. "But I don't understand," Sophia said. The block was empty, only bearing the name of her missing father.

"Lord Sin is growing tired." All six jumped, startled as they turned their attention to the end of the room. Mr. Wheat raised his sword as they all soaked in with uncertainty who had been made aware of their arrival. They beheld two men garbed in long, dark, amethyst hooded robes, each bearing scrolls safely in their hands. Standing between them was the individual who had startled them.

"Lord Sin has directed me to summon your presence," the individual said. Underneath the crimson hooded cloak was a woman tall and slender. Her voice was strong yet smooth, crafting a near hypnotizing tone to its sound. The crimson-cloaked woman spoke. "Come, I shall lead you to Sin." The two men who stood beside her motioned for the group to proceed and follow.

Mr. Wheat and Sophia led the way as their steps echoed throughout the room. An eerie sense breathed upon Sophia's neck as suddenly she thought, "If these great kings, knights, and warriors could not defeat Ri Sin, how can I?" The two men grabbed hold of the iron rings and pulled opened the large oak doors. As the doors opened, the lady cloaked in crimson stepped forward as torch sconces immediately lit as if magnifying her presence. They were unable to catch a glimpse of her face beneath the hood. Her long brown hair was all that was visible to the eye.

"Where is she taking us, Sophia?" asked Savannah as they walked up the stone steps.

"Shh," her sister quickly responded. Again, no one would ever dare believe the tale of these four sisters. Poor innocent Sarah Honey, just at the innocent age of ten, had already overcome far more than great kings of old. She had overcome fowl beasts, the harsh blue cold winter storm, and inhibitors of the Battlefield of Misery. But for what? To be lain before the throne of Ri Sin? Would their efforts ultimately end in vain? Would they too succumb to the supremacy of Olcnom? Sophia continued to hold true to the hope that their journey would not conclude in failure. Just as she had maintained her father's sword, she had no choice but to maintain what little faith she had left. What else did she have while in the bleak halls of Olcnom?

While they walked up the damp, cold steps, the praising chants of the forbidden tongue grew louder and louder as they ascended. Ybbub's heavy breathing almost overshadowed the roar as he tried his absolute best to keep up. The thunderous drums shook the torch sconces along the stone walls as the top had now finally come into view. "Ya know," Ybbub said, "I don't think me homeland has that many steps, even from shore to shore."

As the giant was the last to reach the top, he realized why the others had remained silent. A colossal iron door decorated with thousands of human skulls stood before them. Many still donned barbute, armet, helm, and spangenhelm, armored helmets of war. Some had crowns full of jewels and diamonds laid with silver and gold. A closer look revealed that several were skulls that appeared to be not of man. There were skulls that resembled the likeness of bulls, bears, lions, and even one that appeared to be a well-matured buck. Nevertheless, all of them were an assortment of unfortunate souls taken against their will and presented in the halls of Olcnom. It felt as if the trophies were displayed for a simple warning and declaration to the supremacy that Ri Sin embodied—a declaration as the lord of this kingdom and those he had conquered. He was a self-crowned sovereign whose empire had spread like a cancer in the once-free, joyful world.

The two dark amethyst-clad men turned to the group as they both unraveled their scrolls and read aloud simultaneously. "Behold, Sin lieth at the door!" The racketing of bolts and locks clang from the other side and shook the dust from the ceiling above. The drops of blood began to trickle like rain from the stone walls. An awful sound pierced their ears as the hinges even wailed aloud, pleading for them to turn back from this dreadful place. Never had their hearts pounded so recklessly as they realized this was it. A warm, humid gust of wind blew on them as the crimson-cloaked lady stepped through the threshold first. The blinding flash of bright flames illuminated the gold great helm worn by the old knight as did the hilt of Sophia's father's sword. For the first time on this journey, a thought sprouted within Sophia's innocent, young soul. "I never should have stepped through our cottage door." Now the broad road had led them here, trembling before the terrorizing entry of Sin!

Chapter Twenty-Three

The Vile Face of Sin

The cottage at home was nothing remarkable in anyone's eyes. There were no great towers, lavish marble columns, or priceless stained glass windows. It 'tis not the size or features in general that makes one's home happy though. It is those who indeed reside inside that justify the ingredients for a happy and loving home. Many fall days were spent playing in the woods, running through the fields and just enjoying the simplest blessing in life. Especially in a home with four girls, there were plenty of things to do and plenty of what some would call mischief to plunder into.

Then there were the peaceful, soothing memories that came to mind. The ever-pleasing tune of Mother's angelic voice as she rocked her little daughters to sleep in the late hours of the night still hummed in Sophia's ears. How peaceful and comforting her voice was in that no matter how restless they were, Mother could provide whatever the need may be. On the coldest nights, Father tried his best to keep them warm and cozy as the harsh winter storms blew relentlessly. Home was home, something to truly miss if ever taken away.

As the doors opened wide, Sophia became aware of her sudden misplaced attention regarding her home. As the gates of Ri Sin unbolted, the reality that she was far from her family's cottage was ever more apparent. By the absolute thousands, the earth-shaking roar of the crowd that brooded inside bellowed the sickening chant.

Dee La Dee La Volda Rashka Ri Sin!
Dee La Dee La Volda Rashka Ri Sin!
Dee La Dee La Volda Rashka Ri Sin!

Flames of amethyst and emerald fire burned around a stone courtyard in the shape of a rectangle, extending as far as the eye could visibly see before them. The room was comparable to a coliseum crowded with countless subjects with manlike features. As if rotting with each passing moment, death had passed them by, but they would long for it to escape the stronghold that Lord Sin possessed.

Restless and wild, they all praised their king as their attention fixated upon him who sat in the mote in Olcnom's eye. On the throne, Ri Sin basked in the glory rained upon him by those wretched onlookers. Held with such high mortal repute, this king was not adored by his subjects willfully, but they each held onto life by simply doing so. It 'twas their sole purpose for existence, to praise Lord Sin and extend his realm.

As the group gazed down on Sin's throne from the overlooking door, Olcnom's sovereign sat there unlike any they had seen. Even in the vast distance they could see piles of bones fashioned into a horrendous, coarse throne on which he ruled. On each side of the skeleton frame throne stood two white marble pillars extending up to at least 30 feet. Each had words written in blood—STRIFE and WAR.

At the apex of the marble pillars, great sconces burned high with daunting amethysts and emerald flames. Draped behind the throne was an immense black banner basted with an enormous white sword in which the blade appeared broken and cracked. There was an unmistakable message bearing the calloused certainty of Ri Sin's devotion to break all who dare oppose him. Standing beside the throne were two brute figures wearing black armor dark as the night while donning sallet helmets and battle axes in hand.

The lady in crimson then began walking down the stone steps as the other two ushers gestured for the group to follow behind. The thundering beating of the drums only further intimidated them as they approached the exalted wretched lord of wickedness. Augustus thought it peculiar that they still were granted to bear arms while approaching their favored judge. Could it inevitably be that the small army showed no evidence of the ability to conquer such a nation? Therefore, they were deemed less than unlikely. Their appearance displayed no signs of threat to the high ruler.

Sarah and Scarlett clung to Ybbub. They were unable to settle their emotions due to such an evil, vile place. Closer they came as they reached the bottom of the ancient stone steps. Now in the crest of the stepped valley, they were required to ascend to the throne that led to a flat pedestal. There his majesty resided between the marble columns.

Sophia looked above as she could see the same thick cloud of smoke circling while engulfed with fire and lightning. Another symbol she thought signified what festered inside this awful kingdom. Strife and War—that felt eternal. The black banners waved in the humid wind as the infernos violently flickered atop the columns. Only a few seconds separated them from reaching their adversary they had hunted for the last several days. Five steps remained. Three. Two. One.

Ri Sin sat there unenthused as the lady in the crimson cloak bowed before him along with the amethyst-clad scroll-bearers. They shifted to the right after acknowledging Ri Sin still sitting on the throne of bones. One of the black armored knights shouted aloud as the drums continued to bellow. "Dee La Dee La Volda Rashka Ri Sin!" The skin along his jaw appeared green. His teeth were sharp and filled with hatred while refusing to hide his lust for conflict. The wailing moans mixed with the eerie cadence of the tongues did nothing to comfort the six who stood before Olcnom's lord. Frustration burst from within the black knight as he yelled with a lion's roar, "Dee La Dee La Volda Rashka Ri Sin!" this time directing annoyance to Mr. Wheat as he was in the middle of the line facing the throne.

The other black knight raised his battle axe from the pile of bones and stepped forward while yelling and pointing to the ground. "Bow down to Ri Sin!" All who observed within the coliseum erupted with hatred for the group's disobedience. Mr. Wheat responded with a stern voice. "Aye bow to a no man!"

Overcome with shock, both black knights turned back to Ri Sin in disbelief. The conqueror of kingdoms then sat up on his throne and gently lifted his armor-covered hand. It was a pale, yellowish-covered hand with long black nails, slightly lifted before them. Clad in full black armor, blood ran through its creases and outward like an overflowing basin. Atop his head rested a gold crowned helmet that continued downward covering his face. Much larger than Ybbub himself, Ri Sin towered above them while still sitting on the throne.

The inhibitors of Olcnom ceased their praising instantly as the raised hand threatened their existence if they disobeyed. The crimson-cloaked lady stood there beside him waiting for instructions. Augustus's attention momentarily focused on her face. As the emerald blaze danced upon her red hood, the old knight strained his sight for a closer glimpse of the mysterious cloaked woman. With a voice of a tumbling mountain, Ri Sin spoke. "I am no man! I. AM. SIN!"

In the trenches along the courtyard, flames shot as if fueled by rage. The crowd of cohorts erupted again, banging and beating against the stone walls that secluded them. Spitting, growling, and mocking the group as they stood before Lord Sin, thousands upon thousands praised, acknowledging their ruler. It was a kingdom built on domination and abomination. After days of trials and tribulations, Sin now was ever present before them.

Sophia's next obstacle—where within these putrid, foul walls were her mother and father?

Shades of radiant greens shimmered upon Ri Sin's armor while a black torn cloak draped down his backside. Again, blood spurted out of this fiend as the impurity failed to be dammed by the walls of his yellow cankered flesh. His eyes could be seen through the helmet, which had no pleasant hue or pigment. Solid white were the eyes of Ri Sin, resembling glass marbles filled with suffering smoke. He then raised his hand again as the mockers obeyed the silent command. The two amethyst-cloaked men then unrolled their scrolls and read aloud, "Wide is the gate and broad is the way that leadeth to destruction, and many there be who go in therat!"

The crowned king then eased forward on his throne. Before him stood a shaking giant, a disobedient old man, and four insignificant children. With a voice of a thousand whispers, he spoke. "You seek, do you not? I can give life. I can take it. I can grant. I can deplete. I can sustain. I can desolate. I can open. I can shut. I can do all that you desire. Declare the petition of thine finite soul."

As Sophia stood there with her sisters, she began to wish it were all a dream—even a dreadful nightmare that at any moment her father would wake her up for the morning chores. Could this nightmare be the result of a spoiled cup of milk from Beebone their cow? Could it possibly be the cause of a heavy late-night snack that now lay upon the mind? Nay, but the reality was that she was standing before the one who all had feared for so long.

As she reached down beneath her cloak, she felt the cool hilt of her father's sword. A check of consciousness solidified her apparent situation, the mission they had endured with so many troubles. This was not a nightmare, though that would be far more pleasant than this reality.

One may recall situations in life where spontaneously they responded without thought or inclination—a quick word interjected without a practical thought of disposition. Sophia unexpectedly spoke up. "I have come for my mother and father." Her small, faint voice echoed throughout the colossal throne room, bouncing off the stone walls and into the tortured ears of her mockers and Olcnom's king himself. A request had finally been brought to the king and bestowed at his feet. Still seated, he crouched down to Sophia as his armor discharged its wretched blood from within. Looking her in the eyes, he hissed, "Out of the mouths of babes!" What followed was a discourteous laugh.

The entire castle burst and overflowed with amusement as Savannah and her sisters edged closer to Sophia's side, hoping to comfort their eldest sibling. Ri Sin leaned forward once more to Sophia as the crowd held their tongues. "All you see is rightfully my own," he stated. "Not a jot or tittle exists without my sanction. Strife and War are the hands you see beneath these gauntlets. My child, many of the bones that lay beneath your feet were once mothers and fathers. Entertain me. Give me their names and I will perhaps recall their squeals for mercy before I took their pitiful lives."

Amusement encamped the throne room yet again as the vile king leaned back into the chair, stroked his long black matted hair that lay upon his shoulders, and gave a devilish grin. As all Olcnom laughed, Sophia courageously responded while trying to overcome the thousands in hysteria. "Daniel the Fearless and Noel the Sweet!"

Ri Sin immediately ceased laughing and sadistically rose to his clawed feet. The kingdom hushed as they observed their ruler's countenance change drastically. He quickly looked upon the crimson-cloaked lady in the corner of his eye. Slowly he turned his head and fixed his sight on Sophia. "Thou art the spawn of those pestilences?" The black banner above him waved vigorously as the thick, humid wind blew. Ri Sin's lip snarled, revealing the hatred and loathsomeness that festered inside his miserable being. The curator of death chillingly whispered, "You stand upon their very bones. I have consumed their souls."

Savannah and Sarah's eyes filled with tears in belief that their dear mother and father were no more, tortured and slain by the hand of the vilest, calloused spirit they had ever known. Ybbub bent over as he tried his very best to comfort their broken hearts. Their sobs were uncontrollable as they were overcome with the harsh reality that it was all over.

The terrible silence of their broken hearts was then suddenly interrupted. “Liar!” Bellowing throughout the throne room, Scarlett Bell could no longer contain her frustration and tolerance. As she stood there with Sophia, the little angel lost all restraint regarding the reverence shown by all to Lord Sin. Augustus reached for her as he quietly whispered, “No. Quiet, my a dear. No no no no.”

She pushed Mr. Wheat’s hand aside and shouted, “You lie!” Ri Sin remained speechless as he momentarily paused. With the entire company gazing upon him, he raised his hands and leisurely removed his crowned sallet helmet from his head. The group watched as the crown lowered past his face similar to a grand revealing. This time, though, it was not in excitement or gleeful anticipation. They observed his smoke-filled eyes, his dismal stained teeth that brandished about his mouth, and his scarred yellow skin as if burned by earth’s scorching fires of the deepest flaming pits of Sodom.

All that stood by the throne rapidly fell to their knees as if unworthy to view their lord’s glorious visage. The scroll-bearers, the black knights, and the crimson-cloaked lady bowed before their king. The group of six continued to refuse such reverence.

Ri Sin playfully mumbled, “Bow down to me and I shall give you what your aching heart’s desire.” The drums sounded in the deep as the fire and smoke ravaged their senses that feebly felt tangled within the oppressive web of Ri Sin’s proposal, trapped as a fly in the web at the lone mercy of its fabricator. Upright and waiting for the next broken soul to dine on from his blasphemous palm, Lord Sin sensed he had wisely consumed another. With his smoke-filled eyes, he gazed down upon them, waiting for their shattered spirits to commence worship.

Dee La Dee La Volda Rashka Ri Sin!
Dee La Dee La Volda Rashka Ri Sin!

The chanting adoration had slowly begun once again. Just as the drums pounded in the back, so too did Sophia's thumping heart. *Bow down to Sin? Will he really release Mother and Father? Is it just a trick? Can Ri Sin be trusted?* These thoughts raced in her mind as the palm of evil was extended to her face. Surely she could not feast from the hand offered by the spoken word of Olcnom's vile king. What other choice did she have?

Chapter Twenty-Four

Conquering the Unimaginable

Father once told a story of a young boy he always played with in the village. During the summer they would often spend days in the deep woods, swimming the crystal-clear rivers and venturing into what he claimed were griffin nests. Many of the elder folk would often say that if you find a griffin's nest, you'll find gold. Father said he and his friend climbed to the top of a mountain one day and thought they had found a true griffin's nest. As they both looked down into the deep, brushy pit, he warned his friend not to jump inside the nest for fear of what may be at the bottom. Ignoring Father's advice, his friend blindly jumped into the nest.

"Gold, Dainiel! It's here!" his friend shouted. Then an awful shriek echoed from within. He was struck by a large, venomous serpent that had been lying in wait for the griffin to return. Father quickly lowered a rope down to his friend, who barely made it back to the village alive. The ignorance of the warning my father attempted to give his friend cost him his leg and almost his life. He paid no thought to the serpent that was down in the deep—only the desired treasure he wholeheartedly wished to finally possess.

That tale struck Sophia's mind while standing there before Ri Sin as he awaited her decision. Bow down and receive what your heart desires. Not gold in this case, but mortal man's true treasure . . . family. After all those years, could it be that maybe this is why Father told her that story, to be aware of the serpent while seeking what you long for in life?

"No! I will not bow!" Sophia said as she looked into the eyes of Ri Sin. The crowd faded their chants as the disobedient response shook their loyal souls. Augustus placed his hand on her shoulder while still clinging to the Blade of Despair. Without a word from his lips, Sophia knew that the old Captain approved of her bravery while facing the very monster that slew his beloved son many years ago.

"My dear sweet child," said Sin with a malevolent smile. "Let not your journey be concluded in vain." While his eyes stared deep within her soul, Sin shouted aloud, "Na nat du craz imbe! Bring them forth and cast them at my feet." Suddenly wailing and cries of hundreds filled the throne room as an iron door was lifted. Beneath the stone floor, three guardsmen with faces like wild boars brought forth two unrecognizable individuals. Tattered, bruised, bloody, and without hope they appeared. Bound with no chains or shackles, the only bondage they felt was the imprisonment of Olcnom and the effects thereof.

The lady in the crimson cloak met the guardsmen and escorted the two individuals to the throne. As she passed by, Mr. Wheat finally caught a glimpse of her face beneath the red veil. His eyes opened wide in shock as his knees began to buckle. "Co . . . lit'l Connie!" She turned her head slightly toward him as her bloodshot eyes met his. He felt as if the world had been lifted from about his shoulders. He had finally found his little girl. "Connie! It's a me! Aye, it's a your papa!"

The crimson-cloaked lady responded with not a word, only the sharp refusal not to harken pleasure to the endearing father. Unbeknownst to her, he was her father who had been searching for his little girl for so many grueling years. As she turned her back to him, Augustus pulled the crimson ribbon from his pocket and held it up as his hand vigorously shook. Standing before the throne of Sin, the old man had found what his heart's treasure longed for. "Connie, look! It's a your ribbon! It's a me, papa!"

Ri Sin rewarded no attention to the old broken man as he was absorbed by the little girl's prayer that was granted by none other than himself. Pleased with the condition they were in, he beheld the trifled faces of the four little girls. An evil fiend one must be if the sorrowful tears of children bring joy. The crimson-cloaked lady gestured for the two individuals to be cast at Sin's feet below the throne. "Mother! Father!" Savannah shouted as Sarah Honey was filled with terror. The company of Olcnom all chuckled as they feasted on the grief they witnessed.

"Children . . . uh!" Sweet Noel mumbled in pain as Daniel shouted, "It will all be okay. Don't worry, girls."

Ri Sin then sat back down upon his throne and instructed for their heads to be placed along his feet. "By refusing to bow, I shall make what you long for my footstool." He then placed his rotting feet upon both of their heads as his filthiness ran over them. They both screamed in anguish as they began to feel the pressure of Sin on their skulls.

Watching in horror, Savannah and Scarlett begged for Lord Sin to stop. It was all in vain due to their cries being unfortunately ignored. Paying them no mind, Sin gazed at Sophia. As he bore a wicked smirking grin, he whispered and pointed toward the bone-covered ground. "All you have to do . . . is . . . bow." Scarlett had enough as she attempted to rush toward them, but Ybbub thankfully held her firmly in his clutch. His heart broke for them as he watched their mother and father tortured within Sin's grasp. "Let them go!" Scarlett shouted as the tears rolled down her face, joining many others who had fallen previously in the same spot.

Sophia shook as she stood there hearing her entire family wail in suffering. The tears swiftly dropped from her eyes as she stood frozen, containing a hostile battle within about what to do. Bow or not.

Ri Sin opened his mouth yet again, "The spawn stands

before me, he who hath caused me much affliction in times past. Nigh is the time that his wages shall be recompensed. I have conquered many nations, kings, and soldiers whose remains are displayed in the halls of my courtroom. Bow or you, too, shall join them." As Sophia felt herself yield to his supremacy, she began to slightly bend to the ground. As if her whole world crumbled around her, she heard a shout. "No, Sophia! Do not bow!"

Ri Sin raised himself from the throne, increasing the weight that rested upon Daniel and Noel's heads. The crowd erupted with sickening pleasure as if watching in thrilling entertainment while the chanting tongues roared louder and the drums increased. The emerald flames grew higher, and the black banner bearing the fragmented white sword between the two columns appeared much more present than before.

Sophia turned, seeing her sisters in hysteria and weeping as they clung to Ybbub who also had tears in his eyes. She looked to Mr. Wheat as he slowly removed his helmet from his head. He gave her a look of undeniable defeat, the glaring image of not knowing what to do. Defeated he felt, and it showed. Mr. Wheat lifted the crimson ribbon toward the cloaked lady, gave it a kiss, and gently placed it back in his pocket—a sign of everlasting love to his little girl. Her lips quivered as if her soul melted like sugar. She bowed her head to conceal such mortal sentiments. Love had long been extinguished and replaced by desires of lust, covetousness, and supremacy.

"BOW DOWN!" Lord Sin roared like a thundering lion, taking his fists and slamming them down upon the arms of the throne chair. Having allotted exceedingly more time than he saw fit, Olcnom's Ruler had been prolonged enough. Such disobedience will not be tolerated. Sophia's entire body began to shake as her hand touched the cool, smooth hilt of her father's blade. With uncertainty and the fate of her entire family in Sin's palm and beneath his feet, she miserably felt herself sluggishly lower to the foot of the crown.

As Sin's devilish grin widened about his vile face, much pleasure abode in the bowels of the land's most evil one. He lifted his eyes toward the sky as he laughed her to scorn. "Olcnom! Be it known, there is none who can conquer your king!" All within the throne room became quickened as they perceived another defenseless soul bound by the web of Ri Sin's bondage.

Just before Sophia's knee touched the bone-laden floor, a familiar sound hearkened outside the castle. The coliseum's rumble fell silent as Ri Sin's expression transformed promptly. He lowered his head and directed his attention to his almost devotee, Sophia. She raised herself back up with a look of upheaval about her face. Another blaring echo outside the castle resounded as the thunderous blast shot from ear to ear. It was not a declaration, decree, or sounding from within the realm of Olcnom . . . but from outside.

Mr. Wheat turned to Ybbub and said aloud with a lifted spirit, "Aye yi yi! Da steer horn of Golgrathia!" A smile bloomed as the giant's distressed facade faded into a hopeful heap. "Well, call me Finn McCool!" he whispered.

One of the two amethyst-clad scroll-bearers scurried to the foot of Sin's throne and frantically murmured, "Golgrathia! Your majesty, it's the Royal Golden Eagle Army of the Righteous Kingdom! They are here!"

Lord Sin turned back to Sophia while his feet still pressed against her mother and father's skulls. "Nay! No army shall conquer the hand of Sin! I hold all in my grasp. Life . . . and death!" He lunged toward Sophia as he leaned down from his high throne and reached to grab her by the throat. As the hand of death stretched forth, something sprouted within her. Swift as chain blue lightning, she rolled under the behemoth's clutch, withdrew her father's sword in an instant, and plunged it through the bottom of his jaw. While clinging to the hilt of her father's sword, she noticed the gold as it shined in the malice of the curator's desolate shadow.

Sin let out an awful gurgle as the thick blood ran down onto Sophia's already scarred hands. Olcnom's king raised his feet from atop her mother and father's heads. Sophia still clung to the hilt of the sword. Her feet rose from the ground as Ri Sin pulled the blade from his jaw, knocking her to the now bloody floor. The sword fell as its sound rattled an ear-piercing sting. Speechless were the onlookers as they beheld their wounded sovereign. The black knights rushed forward with their battle axes as Ybbub and Mr. Wheat met them with one last contest for themselves. Ri Sin firmly grasped his wound with one hand as he desperately stretched forth with the other to capture his underestimated adversary. Daniel and Noel quickly crawled from beneath his throne and darted to the other three girls who stood back.

Time slowed as Sophia beheld the sword lying on the stone floor. Appearing lost just as it did the night her beloved parents disappeared, its vacancy became bothersome to her in an instant. Its rightful place was in her hand. No others! She reached down for the sword as Ri Sin wrapped his hand around her waist and gave a quenching squeeze. As her feet dangled in the air, her father and mother ran to try to pull her back, but to no avail. Sin mumbled an appalling gurgle as he held his neck. "That blade is mine. For it shall be broken . . . just . . . as . . . you! As . . . your father! Just as all the kingdoms . . . of this world! None shall conquer me and that which I have built!"

Sin then lifted her high into the air as his smoke-filled eyes crumbled her pure, innocent soul. She heard the cries of her sisters as they watched the life fade from her helpless body. With her father's sword now in hand she refused to let go even while in such pain and agony. She attempted to wield it, but the clutch of Sin was too powerful. Suddenly a flash of a shadow ran across the stone throne room, followed by an abrupt grind of iron against iron. Uncontrollably she fell limp to the floor. Dazing her consciousness, she raised her head back up toward the throne and beheld the crimson-cloaked lady holding one of the Black Knight's battle axes. Her hood was now pulled back as her countenance glistened and flames flashed about her face of beauty. With tears such as blood rolling down her cheeks, she had struck Ri Sin's right arm, piercing through his armor and completely severing it from his body. The severed arm of Lord Sin rattled down the steps as his gauntlet dropped on the floor, rolling distantly from the merciless judgment seat of Ri Sin.

Sophia quickly rose to her feet as the embodiment of wickedness fell to his knees. Staggering there before his throne seat, his subjects now observed their great king wounded by the hands of two women. Sophia gave a shrill yell. "Sin shall conquer no more!" She took her father's sword and rammed it into Sin's chest plate. The blunt, chipped blade barely penetrated his armor as he arrogantly gave her a devilish grin while blood ran down his neck. Fright overtook her childlike complexion as the blade was now seemingly stuck inside, preventing her from delivering a fatal blow.

Suddenly a force from behind knocked her forward, causing the blade to advance farther. Then another jolt! Looking back, she saw it was her two sisters, Savannah and Scarlett. They pushed her with all their might with their dresses flowing in the humid breeze as the blade traveled through the yellow canker chest of Ri Sin. A gurgling growl exploded from his fangs as he extended his forked tongue to them. Sophia then felt another force from behind. It was the youngest of the four, Sarah Honey. The sword had finally pierced the heart of Ri Sin. His eyes, once white as thick smoke, had become black just like his now-impaled heart. What entire kingdoms, present and old, had sacrificed to accomplish had now been achieved by an army of four little girls—four unlikely conquerors.

The girls pulled and yanked the sword from Sin's chest, falling backward over the top of one another. The blade was covered in the black poison from within the embodiment of sin itself. The crimson-cloaked lady sprinted to them and helped them to their feet. "You must hurry! Quick, this way!" She grabbed them by the hand and began to lead them down the stone steps. The King's scroll-bearers shouted aloud as they pointed to the group that fled from the throne of Ri Sin.

"Children of Olcnom, avenge your King!" Mr. Wheat shouted. "Ybbub, quick dis way!"

The giant effortlessly tossed three of the guardsmen into the emerald flames. "Believe I've had enough of this banter for now!" Assisting Daniel and Noel to their feet, Ybbub carried them under his barrel-sized arms while following the others.

Mr. Wheat struggled to keep up with them since he was in pain from his own arm being severed only a few hours earlier.

"Hurry, this way," the crimson-cloaked lady instructed as a blast from above shook the entire castle. The thick, circling cloud of smoke, fire, and lightning clashed above as if the entire kingdom was about to explode from within. They ran from one chamber to the next. Sconces that were once brightly lit with the glowing emerald flame had begun to dim as if the fuel that kept them alight had started to diminish. Just above their heads, a swarm of ravenous harpies swooped down, obeying the order to hold them, prolonging their escape from the castle. With countenances of women and birdlike bodies, these were truly a staggering sight to behold.

Colliding into their faces, the girls screamed as these creatures pulled their hair, bit their ears, and tried ever so hard to deter their departure. Ybbub reluctantly dropped Daniel and Noel when he became the first victim of their hindering siege. Daniel gathered his strength, ripped the sleeve from his ragged tunic, and picked up a large bone lying on the stone floor. Wrapping the fabric around the bone, he ran to the dwindling sconce just above and made himself a brightly lit torch. "Back! Back!" he shouted while violently swinging the bone torch in the air. Screeches and squeals rang throughout the hallways as several of the winged beasts were set ablaze.

Then they faintly heard another discharge of the steer horn from outside the castle. The walls began to shake as the stone steps cracked and shifted beneath their feet. A revolting mob stormed through the dark halls as they sought to destroy the righteous adversaries who had defeated their now-deceased ruler who lay motionless at the foot of his own throne. "There it is!" Savannah yelled as the front iron gate where they had previously entered came into sight.

All dashed to the iron gate as Ybbub yelled, "Help me push! Give it a shove!" The giant placed his pumpkin-sized hands on the iron doors and began to shove with all his strength. The veins became visible about his head as the sweat began to roll down his face. Daniel, Noel, Augustus, and the rest all pushed together. The iron gears began to squeal as they broke free. The door began to crack open while all proceeded to use each ounce of energy they had left.

A cool gust of wind blew through the unfastened crease as Ybbub shouted, "Go! Go! Go!" He then let out a mighty roar as he took one step forward, causing the iron doors to open wider. "Ahhhhh! Hurry!" The girls crawled beneath his tree-trunk-sized legs, running through to the outside. They were followed by Noel and the crimson-cloaked lady, Connie. As the giant, Daniel, and the old knight braced the iron gate open, Ybbub peeked behind him and saw the stone walls commence to cave inward and the wooden timbers above snap. They heard a deafening explosion from above as clumps of fervent fire began to rain down from the vicious circling cloud of smoke.

The ground shook violently beneath them as the gate became even more difficult to hold. The shadows of the wretched children of Olcnom could be seen in the distance, rushing violently toward them as they held the iron gate open.

"Daniel! Hurry! Go!" Ybbub shouted. Daniel hesitated for a moment as he was weaker now than ever before. He lunged through the crack to the other side and attempted to assist again with the gate. Spheres of fire fell from the sky, blocking the nearest route the approaching army could use to try to rescue their captors. Frantically they rode their steeds to try to find a way to assist the giant with their escape.

As the debris and timbers fell by their wayside, Ybbub shouted to Augustus, "Stop ya jiggin' and go, Wheaty! Go on then!" Mr. Wheat hesitated for a moment while still clutching the Blade of Despair with his one hand. Upon barely fitting through the open crack of the door, he shouted, "Come on, Ybbub! Push!" Augustus could see the wicked militia hastening from behind his dear friend, climbing over the wreckage.

The giant shoved with all his might, matching the strength of a hundred men. The hinges buckled as his feet slid in the mud, causing him to fall back several inches while still maintaining what little hold he could. "Ahhhhh! I can't, Augustus! I . . . I can't." Sophia and Daniel rushed to the gate as the marshes within the Battlefield of Misery began to boil around them. Both pulling, they had become aware that they were of no effect. The girls all screamed from afar for their help to miraculously push through the gate and embrace them once more.

Beholding his friend in trouble, Mr. Wheat cast the Blade of Despair behind him and belligerently yanked the door with his one arm. The old man recklessly jerked and yanked as the weight of Sin's gate appeared hopeless and unmovable. "Ahh . . . 'bout my luck! What good is it bein' hearty Gaelic from the isle? Blast!"

The giant gawked at the old knight in the eye while bearing a tender smile. As the legions of Olcnom were now at a stone's cast behind him, he said, "Tell Tootie I'm . . . I'm surry again about them pies." Mr. Wheat slowly stepped back as the tears flowed from the bottom of his helmet and fell to the cold, muddy ground. Lifting his helmet as it rested atop his head, he emerged broken, melting with a grief-stricken sob. The old knight understood what was to come. He had been robbed of so many brave friends in battles, crusades, and war but none that was as close as his dear friend Ybbub.

The gleeful giant cried aloud with a peaceful smile about his face. "Ar scath a cheile a mhaireann na daoine." That is to say, "Under the shadow of each other, people survive." With a trembling lip, Mr. Wheat gave him a loving smile as he brokenheartedly answered, "Aye my a dear friend. Dat we do." The approaching throng of soldiers charged him with lances, axes, and spiked clubs while bearing gruesome intent to destroy. Taking one final peek at the four wholesome lasses as they reluctantly waved goodbye, Ybbub gave a warm, soothing wink, just as he had done from the moment he had met them by the riverside. Sarah waved her hand, and he saw the necklace he had given her was still draped around her neck.

His teeth gnashed together as his countenance changed, bellowing a battle cry that could be heard from miles away. Ybbub shuttered the cumbersome iron doors shut, causing the massive stone walls of Olcnom to plummet inward. The courageous titan had defeated his foes with one resounding blow.

A proud Gaelic giant he was who sported bear hides for his apparel. He was often rumored a quisby but most certainly a brawler when need be. There are no accounts of bare-knuckled fights that he has not been crowned the victor. Many have even considered him a muppet at times throughout his years. But now he will forever be remembered as one whose heart was much larger than his stature. A castle forged by the wicked selfish hands of Ri Sin had been crumbled by the unselfish hands of the Gaelic giant named Ybbub O'Curly.

Chapter Twenty-Five

A Salute to Bravery in the Shadows

The scattered storms of hailing fire had come to an end while the sun unbelievably split through the eastern sky. Only the flames around them were the last malevolent sparks of the trodden, conquered empire that once stood called Olcnom. Its castle lay waste in ruins as the inhabitants shall forever be suppressed, rotting in the pit of the abominable lie of their king. The unveiling truth that following him would ultimately lead them to their demise.

The heavy dust began to settle as the humid air let loose its smothering strangle about their throats. As the wind profusely blew through the brown, ash-covered hair of Sophia, her tranquil attention was still yet upon the fallen kingdom they had narrowly escaped. Suddenly she realized that her mother and father were by her side. They both embraced her.

Savannah, Scarlett, and Sarah Honey all sprinted cheerfully with open arms as the weary family stood safe and sound before the dissolved Kingdom of Olcnom. Tears were now of joy, smiles replaced worrisome expressions, and doubt was overcome with intensified faith.

Mr. Wheat, still gazing at the toppled empire, quietly whispered beneath his breath, "Goodbye, old a friend." He heard crying and quickly turned about. His sweet little Connie ran toward him as she uncontrollably shed tears crafted by thankfulness. The once-curious little girl who became lost in the Black Ghost Forest had finally been rescued. "I thought you'd forgotten about me! I thought you had given up!" she said as her gratitude overflowed while in her father's arms. "No! My lit'l angel. Papa never gave up on a you!"

The steer horn sounded from behind as a prestigious, decorated army stood seamless and readily poised. Hundreds of knights donned in polished golden armor bearing shields and swords lined up steadily. Numerous soldiers sat atop beautiful horses clad with caparisons bearing blue, yellow, and white. Banners whipped in the cool breeze of the wind while bearers' hands held wooden poles firmly. The blue banner featured a golden eagle at the center as two silver swords crossed in its background. With the outskirts trimmed in gold, the sight welcomed peace and comfort to the dreadful Battlefield of Misery.

Mr. Wheat respectfully approached the commanding Knight as he honorably sat atop his snowy white steed. With his glaring armor overlaid by a white, gold-trimmed tunic,

Mr. Wheat recognized his superior rank among the soldiers. Augustus removed the great helm from his head and wiped his brow. While still clinging to the Blade of Despair, the old knight saluted them just as he did many years ago. The commander returned the esteem as he dismounted. Lifting the visor about his basinet, he remorsefully spoke aloud. "Sir! Please accept my dearest apologies regarding our tardiness. I am Commander Byron. Golgrathia has sent two hundred willing souls to rescue your company from the dominion of Olcnom. We hastened as quickly as we could once we received word concerning your requested dispatch, Captain!" Mr. Wheat reassuringly saluted the Commander and said, "Aye. Ya did a fine, Sir. Tank you for a comin' to our aid."

The genuine commander then surveyed the area as he grew confused. "Captain Wheat, where is the rest of your battalion? The rest of your soldiers?" Mr. Wheat smiled as he hobbled over to Sophia and her three sisters and placed his hand on Sophia's head. "Aye. Dey are a right a here. Des lit'l angels are da bravest and a most courageous soldiers aye have a ever waged war beside. Dis is a my army. All accounted for except a fur one. He has perished fur da sake of his comrades." The Commander's jaw dropped as he remarkably complimented the old knight and his allies while bowing before them. "A brave and courageous group indeed, Sir."

Scarlett spoke up and asked Mr. Wheat, "Your dispatch? We never saw you send a letter or dispatch out. How did they know we needed help?" Mr. Wheat laughed as a lieutenant came forward leading Gus by the old, tethered rope that draped about his harness.

"Gus, my a boy! Aye a knew you'd a make it!" Augustus rubbed his faithful donkey's head as his long ears flapped back and forth.

"Wait a minute! What are you talking about?" Scarlett said as she appeared confused, shuffling over to Gus. The donkey turned his head and then gave her a wink along with a whimsical smirk. Sarah Honey laughed as she pointed at Gus and covered her mouth with the other hand. Far too long had it been since the surrounding trees and waters had encumbered such pleasing, chuckling laughter—the laughter of a child. It 'tis still sworn to this day that Sarah Honey's sugary cackles sprang several tulips up from the harsh soil in the once-forsaken Battlefield of Misery. If not, one would most definitely like to believe that to be true. After all, none would trust their tale anyway if ever told of its unachievable achievements.

Solyom suddenly came whispering down from the skyline of the Black Ghost Forest as he eagerly landed atop Mr. Wheat's shoulder. Again, Augustus was comforted to be reunited with his faithful companions. A collective homecoming is what the sight resembled—families painstakingly united through the difficulties that evil had set before them.

Aides then came rushing forth with water and food as they began to care for the group's visible injuries. Although their efforts mended the cuts, scrapes, and even the sweltering pain of Mr. Wheat's lost limb, there was no remedy available for their broken hearts. How does one fill the aching void ripped from their hearts that a tender giant once occupied? Nonetheless, just as their wounds would eventually heal to become scars, so too would the painful gash left from the absence of their warm, benevolent friend.

Sophia looked back at the rubble and then at her family. Unable to comprehend the madness and distress she had just endured, her attention returned to her regained treasure—her family. Her father and mother continually hugged and kissed her and her sisters as smiles were painted about their charred, dirty faces. A soldier then approached them, bearing horses for their journey home. Daniel and Noel, still weak and exhausted, were placed on the horses. Savannah and Sarah mounted together, sharing a horse as did Scarlett and Connie. Commander Byron gave Mr. Wheat the reins to his horse and respectfully insisted that he take his valiant steed. There were two blasts from the steer horn as the soldiers began turning about the line. Gus was tied to the back of Mr. Wheat's horse as their entry back into the depths of the Black Ghost Forest began. In their previous journey, they had hesitantly crept through its vast perils and encountered the creatures contained within whose existence purely exemplified the deed to spoil that which is good. Only six formed the line a day ago as they entered the realm of Olcnom, but an odd feeling came about them all as there were now more than two hundred ready swords offering protection to charge back through.

That valuable peace Sophia sensed was accompanied by the sweet sight of her mother and father. Within herself she thought of so much to tell them regarding their voyage—the tales of stepping through the harsh winter storm tracking the trail in the snow, entering the Black Ghost Forest, the Beo Creatlaches, Belzk, the Stagnus Trees, the Knights of the Broken Wing, the ravaging Verfarka, and so much more. Her stories would have to wait until they arrived home. Sophia was hopeful as they entered the forest that the quest returning would not be as eventful as it was in the beginning. The Black Ghost Forest unwaveringly kept its ice-cold breath upon them as its eerie chill sent shivers down their spines as they crossed through again.

Upon a torturous and long, uncomfortable push through the now seemingly quiet forest, a full day had almost passed. As nightfall was evidently approaching them, the sound of crickets broke the haunting hum of silence as if the choking grasp of evil had loosened its pains upon what little innocence existed inside the woods.

The sounding of a horned bugle echoed near the front of the ranks. The blast woke Savannah who had unintentionally fallen asleep while riding her horse. "Are we there?" she asked. Mr. Wheat cheerfully yelled aloud in response, "Aye my lit'l angel! Dat we are a indeed!" Finally, they arrived back at the Wheats' cottage. The foul-smelling pigs were snorting and squealing, and the cows were mooing brashly. The spooked chickens frantically ran about on their way to roost.

"Lit'l Connie! Lit'l Connie. Look! Dis is where papa and

mama live haha!" Mr. Wheat shouted as the agony that had berated him no longer seemed to have its clench due to his exhilaration at arriving home. The line of soldiers abruptly split into two standard files, forming a secure, somewhat ceremonial wall for the group to travel between. They saw a flicker of light from a candle placed in a lantern near the front of the cottage as it illuminated the outer area of the lovely, cozy home. Gus belted his announcement as did Solyom with a gleeful screech. Both undoubtedly were thankful to ultimately rest their weary legs and wings.

The lantern began to sway as one of the thick, wooden shutters guarding the window crept open. An iron arrow point rested atop a crossbow sticking out of the window crack. It was aimed directly at the Commander who gently raised his hand and announced their presence. "My lady, I am Commander Byron of the Royal Golden Eagle Army sent from the Righteous Kingdom Golgrathia. We have—"

The Commander was immediately interrupted as a loud, discourteous shout came from inside. "Augustus! Is that you?"

Mr. Wheat quickly dismounted from his horse as he shuffled toward the cottage, cheerfully responding, "Aye yi yi my a Tootie! It's me yur a lit'l muffin lump!" The thick, squeaky shutter door swung recklessly open as the resourceful old woman discarded the crossbow and climbed over the window sill to the outside. All watched as the two ran toward one another and embraced, withholding any concern for who may witness their sought-after returning affection.

As the soldiers stood near, each respectfully turned their heads to issue a polite form of privacy to the couple. Her kisses were heard down the line to the last foot soldier standing guard as the great helm helmet rolled about the stone-pebbled roadway. Mr. Wheat's brown arming cap dropped over his brow, covering the old knight's sight. In an instant, the smooches ceased as Mrs. Wheat began to run her palm down the left shoulder of her fatigued and weary husband. There was a change of emotions as Mr. Wheat appeared confused, reached up, and pulled back the arming cap that covered his eyes to view what had caused his dearly beloved to stop their passionate engagement.

Smack! What he saw next was the sight of his dear wife delivering a devastating strike with the palm of her calloused, overworked hand. The old man fell to the ground, flirting with losing consciousness while the entire company observed the embarrassing display of chastisement. He looked up from the ground. Tootie stood over him while yelling obscenities to make even the most vulgar tavern brawler blush. "You stupid, bobolyne, fopdoodle, dimwit!" Connie quickly placed her hands over Scarlett's ears as did Savannah Sarah's. "Bogger, pillock no good lousy twit! What in heavens happened to ya bloody arm?"

Augustus, while still trying to regain his consciousness and dignity, attempted to answer her contritely. "Tootie, aye uh." She began to look around the lines of soldiers as they all grew fearful of the berating, gray-haired female. "Where is he? Where is he? I'll break his nose! I'll beat him 'til he's blue! I told him not to let anything happen to ya! That good-for-nothing giant! Ybbub! Ybbub O'Curly! Come here now!" Mrs. Wheat pointed to the ground with her finger as if calling a mischievous hound back for a well-earned beating. "Ybbub! Now!" Tootie shouted as Mr. Wheat used the Blade of Despair to climb his way back to his feet.

The old woman could see the look about her husband's face, a familiar look that she had observed too many times in their lives when he would return home. "Oh no! Oh no!" She crumbled to her knees as Mr. Wheat comforted her the best he could. Even as the fresh handprint burned across his beaten, soot-filled face, the two were back in each other's arms. As they both mournfully wept, their daughter, Connie, stepped down from her horse and quietly walked over to where they knelt and lovingly placed her hand on the back of her weeping mother whom she had not seen for over twenty years. Tootie raised her head and turned to see who consoled her. As the old woman looked up, her tears of sorrow instantly change into tears of joy. A broken heart stricken with grief had become, within several beats, a heart overcome with joy.

Mrs. Wheat slowly rose to her feet as she stood holding her daughter's face in the palms of her hands. Staring into her eyes, Tootie saw the immoral deeds, destruction, and misery that had chained her daughter for all those years while she was lost. But she unequivocally saw her sweet little girl whom she loved and longed for so many restless, sleepless nights. As the tears ran down both their faces, smiles of gladness blossomed simultaneously. Tootie grabbed her daughter and pulled her in for a long-awaited hug.

Commander Byron approached Daniel and whispered, "Sir Daniel, it may be in our best interests if we continue forward. For we do not know if the enemy shall pursue and follow our course." Daniel lifted his eyes to the swaying tops of the trees that blew in the wind and seemingly paused for a moment. Not 'til now was he able to soak in the blessed freedom he thought he'd never obtain while being chained in the torturous, demented black pits of Olcnom. As he closed his eyes he could hear the joyful laughter of his dear wife and four beautiful children. Their voices were buoyant music beating about his eardrums that lifted his soul merrily. He took a deep breath and nodded in agreement with Commander Byron. "Yes, Sir. But before our departure, I must thank the Wheats for all they have done for me and my family."

Perched upon a branch high in a tree, an owl began to hoot its moonlight call as Daniel hobbled over to Mr. Wheat. He was standing beside his wife and daughter with a look of happiness that Daniel had never seen on the old knight's face. "Augustus, I cannot thank you enough for all that you have—"

Mr. Wheat slowly raised his hand and interrupted him. "Daniel." He then pointed to the four girls standing with their mother, Noel, and petting Gus. "No. Aye must a thank a you. Dos lit'l angels der. Dey are a precious. Precious to me. Dey are da bravest warriors aye have ever had da honor of a fiting with. Dey have a changed dis a old broken man. If a not fur dem, none of dis would a ever a happened. Dey are a why you and Sweet Noel are a free. Dey are da heroes, not a me."

Commander Byron, sitting atop his horse, gave signal for the steer horn to blow. "Sir Daniel! We must be going," he patiently exclaimed. Mr. Wheat saluted Daniel as he, too, honorably returned the much-warranted reverence. "Protectors of the Pure," Augustus whispered. "And Avengers to the Wicked!" Daniel added.

Sophia and her sisters all ran to Augustus and clung to him with a warm, loving hug. "Aye yi yi. My a lit'l angels. You make a Mr. Wheat so a happy!" Sophia looked up at the old man. She could see that sadness and guilt no longer engulfed his eyes. She wrapped her arms around his neck and gave an innocent kiss on his blood-stained cheek. "Thank you, Mr. Wheat! Thank you so much!"

All of them walked back to their horses as they prepared to leave, forming two lines along each side of the trail. As Commander Byron passed by, he shouted aloud beneath his basinet, "Hail Captain Wheat! Protector of the Pure and Avenger to the Wicked!" The two lines of soldiers responded firmly to the command while unsheathing their swords and calling out in cadence, "Hail Captain Wheat! Protector of the Pure and Avenger to the Wicked!" Each glamorous knight passed by, placing their swords across their faces in gestures to salute Mr. Wheat with the upmost esteem. With his loving wife and newfound daughter by his side, the old knight felt the proudest he had ever been at this moment. The thick shadows of the soldiers flickered in the bright moonlight, casting silhouettes over Mr. Wheat and his adoring family. Oddly enough, the last words of his late friend echoed in his weary time-worn mind. "Ar scath a cheile a mhaireann na daoine." That is to say, "Under the shadow of each other, people survive."

Chapter Twenty-Six

A Sword Only Worthy of One

Swiftly swinging back and forth was the old wooden door to their cottage as the rusted iron hinges could be heard from far away. The sun had begun to peek from the ridgetop, awakening from its slumber, all the birds loudly singing their sweet melodies welcoming in the new day. Regal nervously neighed while still nestled inside his stall, calling out to the oncoming horses mounted by the arriving escorting army. Their services may have arrived late by some standards, but these six were just thankful for the pleasant company while traveling home. The soldiers continued as they circled about the cottage, checking the stable, pens, and surrounding area for possible danger that may be hiding as a serpent in the tall grass. Commander Byron along with Sir Kluh entered the cottage to verify a safe entry for its rightful inhibitors.

"Savannah! Wake up! We're home!" Sophia whispered. All night the eldest of the girls attempted to process each unimaginable event that had taken place over the last few days. In doing so, making the half-day (or in their case half-night) journey feel as if it had only taken several minutes—passing back through the eerie Black Ghost Forest and around the river that still laid claim to her dear mother's quilt. It was where the Beo Creatlaches nearly claimed her life if it had not been for that dear old giant. Numb had her mind become, and rest no doubt was what she needed.

"The sword!" Sophia immediately thought while feeling it swiftly down to the hilt as it rested upon her thigh. "Still there." Her heart thumped vigorously like a horse racing along an open field. The young girl had managed to possess it this long. It would have been a tragedy if it were to have slipped through her fingers while pondering all those thoughts along the journey home. *It's still with me*, she said inside her tired and restless mind. That too was true for her family as the two lines all halted, finally arriving at the front door of their cottage.

Soldiers paced over to the family to assist them all from their saddles. Daniel and Noel stood gazing with tears in their eyes, overcome with joy but not yet convinced it was all not a dream while still in the grave dungeons of Olcnom. Commander Byron and Sir Kluh walked back out of the cottage to Daniel and his family. "Sir Daniel," Commander Byron declared, "the cottage appears to be clear with no danger present. We have also started a warm fire inside and have left provisions for you and your family on the table. We pray that these will bless you and your family.

"Oh, bless you! Thank you for all you have done for us," Noel said while wiping the tears from her eyes.

"Is there anything else we may do for you and yours, Sir Daniel?" Sir Kluh asked. Daniel looked back at his four girls as they began walking toward the front steps of the cottage, Sophia in front followed by Scarlett, Savannah, and Sarah Honey. A smile stretched across the face of Commander Byron as he began to chuckle. "My, my, Sir Daniel. I believe no doubt that those four girls could have escorted you and your wife back home better than my men and I."

Daniel patted the top of Sophia's head as she stood next to him. "Aye. I have no doubt at all."

Commander Byron motioned for the steer horn to sound once more as he and his knights all re-formed the two lines to return to the castle. A salute with the sword was given as they all passed by the cottage. The sun now beamed over the mountaintop and through the trees. As its warm rays hit the knight's armor, it appeared as if a street of gold was parading along the pathway back toward the kingdom. While they all stood there waving goodbye, someone asked, "What kind of food did they leave?" Each member of the family turned around as they looked at Scarlett Bell. "What?" She then said. "I'm hungry."

That evening as the night sky fell, all gathered around the warm, crackling fireplace while resting in each of their usual designated areas. Mother sat in her rocking chair humming her angelic tune while holding Sarah Honey. Savannah and Scarlett sat on the floor eating the treats left by Commander Byron and washed them all down with a large cup of cow pull. Daniel and Sophia sat at the table as she finished her cup of cow pull before bed. It was a scene that a day ago they all had momentarily lost faith in doing once more. Precious moments like these are what makes a home a home—the desire to be with one another. One does not know when these little moments will be taken away. *Moments like these cannot be taken for granted*, Daniel thought while sitting there looking at his loving family.

All exhausted and barely occupying enough strength to stay awake, the time had come. "Alright girlies, it's time for bed. Give me a kiss," Mother said as she clung to each of her girls.

"I'm so happy you're home, Mother," Sarah Honey said. "Me too!" shouted Scarlett as she continued to chew a mouthful of biscuits and jam. Each made their way up the stairs after giving Father a tight hug and kiss on the cheek. "Goodnight, dear," Noel said, giving him a loving kiss. She hobbled and shuffled to the bedroom, nearly half asleep and already extending her arms in the air with a tiresome yawn.

"Oh! Wait!" Sophia shouted. "I almost forgot!" She frantically ran up the stairs, sounding like a herd of Stagnus Trees plowing through the forest. A few seconds later she carefully walked back down the steps holding something in her hands. Breathing heavily with her hair now all tangled while in her long gown, she said, "I know this is yours and we're not supposed to touch it. I know who you really are, Father. You're a knight. You're Sir Daniel the Fearless. Mr. Wheat told me all about it. I forgot to give this back to you earlier."

She reluctantly looked down at the ground as if she were about to be punished. Holding her father's sword, she extended it out to him. Reaching out, he gently took it from her hands and held it up in front of his face. Once again the fearless knight noticed the chips, stains, and notches that covered the blade along the pummel. Many were familiar to him and flashed memories in his mind's eye, but some—some he was not so familiar with. Seeing his reflection in the blade while holding it in front of his face, he froze for a moment and then smiled. He lowered the sword and extended it back toward his daughter. Daniel placed his arming sword back in her hands. "No, I am not the one who is fearless. You are. You have conquered far more than I. This great sword no longer belongs to me. It belongs to you now."

Sophia's countenance lit as bright as the stars in the midnight sky as she leaped into her father's arms and gave him a loving hug. As she stepped back, he looked down at her hands while she held the sword and uttered, "Sophia, your hands! How did you get those scars?" She looked up at her father as he gazed down at her wounded palms. The flames from the fire flickered as the flashes showed the most unsettling expression on her face. While reflecting upon them herself, it was as if the searing pain had suddenly come back, feeling the blade slice through her grip as she refused to let go of her father's sword. She took a deep breath and sighed, "It's very late, Father. Let's go to bed."

Acknowledgement

I am convinced that every tall tale must contain some form of truth to it in one way or another. With the completion of my book it is with a thankful heart that many dear family members have influenced me to fashion endearing characters based upon fascinating qualities they all uncommonly possess. From my sweet wife Hannah, my dear little angels Sophia, Savannah, Scarlett and Sarah to my own lifelike giant himself "Uncle Bubby" Robert Phillips. For without these characters in my life and many more, it would not have been possible to bring them to life within the pages of my book. To them all, thank you!

www.ingramcontent.com/pod-product-compliance
Lightning Source LLC
LaVergne TN
LVHW050624100826
845148LV00011B/1727

* 9 7 8 1 6 3 2 9 6 9 7 2 9 *